Stinging Fly Patrons

Many thanks to: Ann Barry, Niamh Black, Denise Blake, Jane Blatchford, Celine Broughal, Trish Byrne, Edmond Condon, Evelyn Conlon, Sue Coyne, Liam Cusack, Michael J. Farrell, Michael Gillen, Helene Gurian, Brendan Hackett, Nuala Jackson, Claire Keegan, Jerry Kelleher, Conor Kennedy, Ruth Kenny, Gráinne Killeen, James Lawless, Joe Lawlor, Irene Rose Ledger, Wendy Lynch, Róisín McDermott, Petra McDonough, Lynn Mc Grane, Finbar McLoughlin, Maggie McLoughlin, Dan McMahon, Ama, Grace & Fraoch Mac Sweeney, Mary Mac Sweeney, Paddy & Moira McSweeney, Anil Malhotra, Marian Malone, Helen Monaghan, Christine Monk, Dáirine Ní Mheadhra, Joseph O'Connor, Nessa O'Mahony, Maria Pierce, Peter J. Pitkin, Orna Ross, Fiona Ruff, Peter Salisbury, Eileen Sheridan, Brian Smyth, Peter Smyth, Karen, Conor & Rowan Sweeney, Mike Timms, Olive Towey, Simon Trewin, The Irish Centre for Poetry Studies, Munster Literature Centre, Poetry Ireland and Trashface Books.

We'd also like to thank those individuals who have expressed the preference to remain anonymous.

By making an annual contribution of just 50 euro, patrons provide the magazine and press with vital support and encouragement.

Become a patron online at
www.stingingfly.org
or send a cheque or postal order to:
The Stinging Fly, PO Box 6016, Dublin 1.

The Stinging Fly
new writers, new writing

Editor
Declan Meade

Poetry Editor
Eabhan Ní Shúileabháin

Design & Layout
Fergal Condon

Editorial & Admin
Thomas Morris

Eagarthóir filíochta Gaeilge
Aifric Mac Aodha

Contributing Editors
Emily Firetog, Dave Lordan & Sean O'Reilly

© Copyright remains with authors and artists, 2012
Printed by Hudson Killeen, Dublin
ISBN 978-1-906539-23-8 ISSN 1393-5690

Published three times a year (February, June and October). We operate an open submission policy. Guidelines on page 114 and on our website: www.stingingfly.org

The Stinging Fly gratefully acknowledges the support of The Arts Council / An Chomhairle Ealaíon and Dublin City Council

PO Box 6016, Dublin 1
stingingfly@gmail.com

DUBLIN BOOK FESTIVAL

SMOCK ALLEY THEATRE

TEMPLE BAR

13–18 NOVEMBER 2012

Free Events, Discussions, Debates, Readings, Children's Events

Featuring: Kevin Barry, Dermot Bolger, John Bowman, Harry Clifton, Mary Costello, Diarmaid Ferriter, Declan Hughes, Jennifer Johnston, Mike McCormack, Oisín McGann, Jimmy Magee, Neven Maguire, Dervla Murphy, Éilís Ní Dhuibhne, Nuala Ní Chonchúir, Dr Eva Orsmond, Sheila O'Flanagan, Fintan O'Toole, Feargal Quinn, Patricia Scanlan, Alice Taylor, John Waters and many more.

Full programme available at:
www.dublinbookfestival.com

issue 23/volume two
Winter 2012-13

RE:FRESH

| 8 | Mary Costello | 'My Lord You' by James Salter |

NEW FICTION

16	Fiona O'Connor	*Always the Stranger*
30	David Hayden	*Return*
40	Gina Moxley	*Transition*
49	Suzanne Power	*Pilgrimage*
63	S.J. Ryan	*Main Street, Underworld*
74	Claire-Louise Bennett	*Morning, 1908*
83	Tania Hershman	*Fine as Feathers*
89	Colin Corrigan	*I Can Do This*
97	John O'Donnell	*Ostrich*
104	Danielle McLaughlin	*Night of the Silver Fox*

FEATURED POET

| 24 | Tadhg Russell | Nine poems |

NEW POEMS

6	Grace Wells	*The Pain Index of Writer's Block*
14	K.V. Skene	*Once A Blue Moon*
15	Victoria Kennefick	*Moby-Dick*
36	Joe Dresner	Two poems
38	Ted Deppe	*The Lost Notebook*
46	Haris Vlavianos	Two poems – translated by Evan Jones
48	Ruth Padel	*Mill Wheel At Bantry*
56	Janet Shepperson	Two poems
58	J. Roycroft	*Homily (or The Odd Couple)*
60	Elaine Feeney	*Mass*
80	Clare McCotter	*The Black Lark*
82	Lou Wilford	*Six Months*

NEW POEMS (CONTINUED)

85	Fran Lock	*When the world ends*
88	Nicola Griffin	*Security*
94	Sally Rooney	*The Stillest Horse*
96	Carolyn Jess-Cooke	*The Waking*
102	Paul Perry	*August 30, 2012*

COMHCHEALG

68	Stiofán Ó Cadhla	*Dhá dhán*
70	Seán Mac Mathúna	*Fuascailt Nell Crane*

REVIEWS

115	Gerard Smyth	*The Ash and the Oak and the Wild Cherry Tree* by Kerry Hardie
		Fireflies by Frank Ormsby
119	Sara Baume	*Replacement* by Tor Ulven
121	Kevin Breathnach	*Winter Journal* by Paul Auster
		A Death in the Family by Karl Ove Knausgaard

COVER PHOTOGRAPHY

Fionán O'Connell

COVER DESIGN

Fergal Condon

'... *God has specially appointed me to this city, so as though it were a large thoroughbred horse which because of its great size is inclined to be lazy and needs the stimulation of some stinging fly...*'
—Plato, *The Last Days of Socrates*

Next Issue Due: February 2013

The Pain Index of Writer's Block

After the Schmidt Sting Pain Index

'I've always been blocked as a writer but my desire to write has been so strong that it has always broken down the block and gone past it.'—Tennessee Williams

0.2   Mild irritation, like losing a thought
on the tip of your tongue.

1.0   Perpetual frown, as if straining liquid
through a sieve partially clogged
with pips and seeds.

2.5   An unexpected sense of loss and injustice
comparable to standing naked by the bath
and finding there's no hot water.

3.8   Nagging exasperation, similar to being
stuck in rush-hour traffic
on a wet Friday in December.

4.6   Growing malcontent, like having a mouse
living in the walls of your bedroom
and being unable to trap it.

5.0   Frustrating sense of isolation akin
to the second day of a cold, head
congested, eyes streaming.

5.5   Turgid constriction, picture a gutter
        choked with decayed and foul-smelling leaves.

6.0   An ongoing, season-long suppression of spirit.

7.2   A slow-burning injustice in the bones like being
        sent to the Gulag for a crime you did not commit.

8.5   Life-threatening, tempestuous pain. Imagine
        a dolphin thrashing in a net off Taiji, Japan.

9.0   The windpipe has closed. You live without air.

10.0   Elements of all of the above, combining
        to numb the body: the paralysis
        of observing years pass and not sitting down
        to that first precious word.

Grace Wells

RE:*fresh* | 'My Lord You' by James Salter
Mary Costello

It is a summer's evening. Ardis, the young wife in James Salter's story 'My Lord You', and her husband Warren are attending a fashionable party in a house on Long Island. They are among the beautiful and the bright. There is a veranda, sea light, caviar and as dusk falls the company moves indoors. The mood is languid, and everything—the guests, the setting, the conversation—is cool and elegant and seductive. So far, so good, so Salter. Then, enter Brennan, a drunken poet: handsome, arrogant, dishevelled—a man 'used to being ungovernable'. To Ardis's alarm he seats himself beside her. 'I know who you are, another priceless woman meant to languish.' Were men drawn to you when they knew they were frightening you? she wondered. For a moment his talk is tender. He quotes from Ezra Pound. He describes his first sighting of his now estranged wife. 'She was walking on the beach. I was unprepared. I saw the ventral, then the dorsal. I imagined the rest. Bang. We came together like planets. Endless fornication.' Ardis is riveted. Warren stands close by, nervously pushing his glasses up on his nose with one finger. Before Brennan can be steered back out into the night he calmly reaches out a hand, mid-sentence, and touches Ardis's breast. 'She was too stunned to move.'

There is an immense erotic charge. This loose cannon, this reckless semi-feral man, both disturbs and arouses Ardis, opening a portal into her unlived life. Days after the encounter she goes to the library, seeks out the poem from which he quoted: 'The River Merchant's Wife', Pound's interpretation of an eighth-century Chinese verse, in which a young wife yearns for her absent husband:

> At fourteen I married My Lord You.
> I never laughed, being bashful.
> Lowering my head, I looked at the wall.
> Called to, a thousand times, I never looked back.

In Ardis's life there had been only one My Lord You, when she was twenty-one. She recalls their love-making in an apartment on 58th Street, hot afternoons, the room filled with slatted light. She called him several times over the years, foolishly believing that love never dies.

Later in the story, as she cycles home from the beach, Ardis cannot help herself from detouring by Brennan's house. She walks her bicycle up the long driveway, watching the house, aware of the forbiddenness of her actions. No one is home. 'She walked farther. Suddenly someone rose from the side porch. She was unable to utter a sound or move.'

It is a dog, a huge deer-hound, yellow-eyed, coming towards her, higher than her waist. She has a fear of dogs. She manoeuvres the bicycle between herself and the animal. *Good boy, good boy* is all she can manage. He is moving like a machine and her legs and calves are there, bare, ready to be ripped open. She gets up on the bicycle, cries 'No! No!' and obediently he veers off. She cycles away, free, and when she turns her head he is following in the fields, on fire in the sun, floating alongside on large lumbering limbs.

James Salter was born in New York in 1925 and spent twelve years in the US Air Force before leaving to pursue a writing career. He wrote film and TV scripts for Hollywood and his first novel, *The Hunters*, based on his air force experience in Korea, was made into a movie in 1958. His best known novel, *A Sport and a Pastime*, is a tender erotic story—where sex comes with love—set in provincial France. *Light Years* charts the life of a married couple in New York and the deep dark currents of their love and infidelities. The stories in his two collections *Dusk* and *Last Night* are tense, taut, immaculate. Each word is weighed, and the real and ordinary are elevated to a state of beauty and pleasure. Salter is a master of mood, and stillness. There is a feel of lushness, yet the writing is never lush—I don't know how he does this—but beautifully distilled and aching with suggestion. He does women well, gets them so right. He conveys with exquisite delicacy and a dreamlike quality their sensuality, their intense private longings, their pining for love or sex, and does so with an empathy and understanding that is rare among his contemporaries. In *Light Years* he gives equal accent to the body and carnal life of the wife, Nedra, as he does to that of Viri, the husband. Perhaps even more. Crucially he does not, nor do the characters themselves, seek to blame their men for the shortcomings and regrets that attach to their lives. Instead, he allows the reader to absorb with terrible poignancy the elusiveness of deep human connection, and the temporary nature of both physical and psychic union.

That night, in the bedroom after making love with her husband, Ardis senses something. In the morning the dog is on the lawn, under the trees, 'its forelegs stretched out in front like a sphinx, its haunches round and high'. The next day the dog is there again, waiting for her. She approaches him, sensing his power, but also his abandonment. 'Come,' she says and he follows her down the road to Brennan's house. Brennan has still not returned. The dog is starving. She tries the porch door—it is unlocked. She enters and walks around—she is in the house of a poet, an artist. In every room books, abundance, disregard. Loose pages on a desk, lines of a newly minted poem. Photographs of his wife, more lines: *Tus besos.* Your kisses. She wanders through the forbidden rooms, carried away. In the bathroom she stands, and the dog comes to the door, falls to the floor before her.

'She turned to him. All she had never done seemed at hand.'

And then, her shocking act. She begins to remove her clothes. She strips to the waist: '… dazzled by what she was doing. There in the silence with the sunlight outside she stood slender and half-naked, the missing image of herself, of all women. The dog's eyes were raised to her as if in reverence. He was unbetraying, a companion like no other. She remembered certain figures ahead of her at school. Kit Vining. Nan Bondreau. Legendary faces and reputations. She had longed to be like them but never seemed to have the chance. She leaned forward to stroke the beautiful head.'

Ardis, the good schoolgirl, the meek little wife, dares to be what she has always longed to be—full and whole and reckless. The act is spellbinding, a moment of stunning sensuality, and absolute abandon. The dog is audience, witness, a real and symbolic figure of masculine potency and danger, a substitute Brennan. She is half-naked before him, exposed and vulnerable—and a woman stripped to the waist is even more vulnerable, more defenceless somehow, than one fully naked. She is submitting to the dog, to Brennan, to all men, but more: she is sating a private hunger, an ache in her body, in her breasts, surrendering to the wildness in herself. 'You're a big fellow,' she says, kneeling and stroking his head again and again.

When I first read this story I was completely arrested. I was not surprised to learn that Salter is a dog-lover (though now at eighty-seven, he no longer keep dogs) but one need not be a devotee to feel the depth of the connection here, the melt of animal love. At the heart of the story is Ardis's inner awakening and while Brennan is the catalyst, the physical embodiment of man who stirs up her desire, it is the dog who is her agent of change, her psychopomp. He is an aspect of her animus—the masculine principle laid down and embedded in the blueprint of every woman's psyche. In his sheer physicality, with his yellow eyes and machine-like capability, he is a potent presence, a wild creature that could, in the blink of an eye, rip her to pieces. He embodies the instincts she fears and suppresses in herself. Yet, when forced, she can tame this wildness, call him to heel with a *No!* and later, *Come!*, and integrate her own polar instincts—power and weakness, fear and trust, desire and passivity, which the dog possesses, for he is, too, gentle, unbetraying, 'a companion like no other.' Woman and animal break through to each other. Ardis is edging towards something and it is in this human-animal encounter that she comes to a knowingness, a way of being that goes beyond the physical. It is the animal gaze, the humming of his animal soul—reminiscent of Ted Hughes' jaguar and Rilke's panther, but more significantly of Rilke's notion of the 'open'—that tips Ardis into this moment of pure luminous joy, into an awareness of their shared creatureliness, something that existed before time, before words, or as Rilke puts it:

> … within the wakefully-warm beast
> there lies the weight and care of a great sadness.
> For that which often overwhelms us clings
> to him as well—a kind of memory
> that what one's pressing after now was once
> nearer and truer and attached to us
> with infinite tenderness.

In no man, in no other human, will Ardis encounter such tenderness, such relatedness, or be afforded a glimpse into the 'open'. She has begun to see with her animal eyes, feel with her animal heart.

'With all its eyes the creature-world beholds the open.' This 'open' in Rilke's *Duino Elegies*—and especially in the eighth elegy—encompasses the whole of external reality, nature, and the unseen reality of all worlds, all realms. Rilke thought that children and the dying have access to it, but while lovers come close each blocks the other's view:

> Lovers – were not the other present, always
> blocking the view! – draw near to it and wonder…
> Behind the other, as though through oversight,
> the thing's revealed…

The rest of us are mere spectators, never totally at one with 'the thing', lacking the sensory faculty to perceive it. But it is animals, it is the dumb brute who is capable of being fully in the 'open', of seeing everything in each moment:

> … for it
> is infinite… pure, like its outgazing.
> Where we see Future, it sees Everything,
> itself in Everything, for ever healed.

And so back to Ardis in the bathroom, kneeling, stroking, submitting, when suddenly from outside there is a crunch of tyres on gravel to bring her abruptly to her senses. Brennan. She throws on her clothes and rushes out. It is her husband, come to find her. *Thank God, she thought helplessly*. An awkward guilty moment ensues.

That evening the wind rises, the elements conspire, the sea breaks through to a pond. And the dog returns, slow, weak. She cannot bear it. She carries out a bowl of water, kneels before him ceremonially, her hair blowing in the wind, like a mad person. His gaze drifts away. His eyes are almost closed. Night comes, the wind blows itself out. In the early morning the dog is still there but something—his shape—is different. He is dead. She runs out in her nightdress, barefoot, across the wet grass:

> She took a step or two forward. She could sense the heavy limp weight that would disperse, become something else, the sinews fading, the bones becoming light. She longed to do what she had never done, embrace him. At that moment he raised his head.

It is miraculous. She turns. *Warren!* she cries. The shouts distress the dog and he rises wearily and slopes off.

> She ran after him. Warren could see her. She seemed free. She seemed like another woman, a younger woman, the kind one saw in the dusty fields by the sea, in a bikini, stealing potatoes in bare feet.

Ardis never sees the dog again. She goes by the house many times and though Brennan's car is there, there is no sign of the dog. Her loss is immense. But she will return to her husband and her life, and nothing in her outer bearing will give any indication of what she has suffered or how she has been altered.

Each time I read this story I am spellbound, rapt. As it unfurls a weight slowly descends on the heart but I am repeatedly drawn back to Ardis and the dog, addicted. I feel their presence, utterly.

I am reminded of Camus's story 'The Adulterous Wife', and how it too arrests and induces the same weighted heart. At its centre, another dead woman walking. Set in Algeria, Janine and her salesman husband Marcel, a childless couple in their forties of French extraction, travel by bus out of the capital, Algiers, into the desert on business. On the bus Janine observes the Arab men with their sunburnt faces and burnooses. She has a brief silent encounter with a French soldier, prompting a recollection of her youth and an awareness of her present body's fleshiness and waning attraction. Love takes many forms and while, like Ardis and Warren, this couple is not entirely devoid of love, it is a dull feeble love. Barely love at all. Certainly not love in its fullest, most extreme manifestation.

The couple overnight in a village and the next evening they climb to the roof of a military fort and Janine views the rugged landscape and the sky and, in the distance, a nomad encampment. The place affects her deeply. That night, in the cold, she sneaks out of the hotel room and runs along the street and climbs to the roof of the fort again. She gazes around, her heart beating wildly, feels the desert and the night mingling, hears voices from the camps in the distance, remembers the dark faces of the Arab men—mysterious, primitive, free. She looks up, and the sky seems to gyrate and thousands of stars fall one by one from the black night, extinguishing themselves in the stones of the desert, 'and each time Janine opened a little more to the night.' She forgets the cold, the struggle of life, the weight of humanity.

> Pressing her whole belly against the parapet, leaning against the wheeling sky, she was only waiting for her pounding heart to settle down, for the silence to form

> in her… Then, with an unbearable sweetness, the waters of night began to fill Janine, submerging the cold, rising gradually to the dark centre of her being, and overflowing wave upon wave to her moaning mouth. A moment later, the whole sky stretched out above her, as she lay with her back against the cold earth.

It is a numinous moment and she is exalted, transformed, liberated from her weeping inert self. Her adultery is not with any living man but with nature and the night and all of mankind—with the universe itself—as she surrenders to this metaphysical union and to a physical and psychical reawakening.

This is philosophical fiction and what Janine and Ardis are hungry for—and what they stumble upon in the course of their 'adulteries'—goes beyond the physical or sexual, beyond earthly love. Salter and Camus have given their women a deeper reach, a solitary quest for something that no man—husband or lover—could possibly embody or provide for a woman, and vice versa. It is the aspiration, the urge, the hunger to go into the pure space of Rilke's 'open'. In the everyday Ardis and Janine yearn for an essential life, for the quiver and tremble of copious primal love. Both are 'unfaithful' and in their consummation with nature, sky, the night, they are given the taste, the thirst for something transcendental and they are both saved and ruined and there will be no going back for them, ever.

In the final scene of 'My Lord You' when the dog is resurrected at dawn and disappears, Ardis is bereft. She will never see him again. Salter tells us that the dog may be gone '—lost, living elsewhere, his name perhaps to be written in a line someday though most probably he was forgotten, but not by her.'

Ardis is changed, 'a thing's revealed', but Salter does not remove the weight of her soul-suffering or her grief for the dog. That then would be a different story. Salter knows that we cannot overcome the human condition, that the most we can do is acknowledge it, face it, sometimes embrace it. In his essay, 'The Wind at Djemila', Camus wrote:

> Everything people suggests seeks to deliver man from the weight of his own life. But as I watch the great birds flying heavily through the sky at Djemila, it is precisely a certain weight of life that I ask for and obtain. When I am at one with this passive passion the rest ceases to concern me.

Ardis and Janine would, no doubt, wish to be delivered from the weight of their lives too but in their encounters with the poet and the dog, with the soldier and the night—and in their abandon—they are made to feel that certain weight and feel it intensely. They venture further and deeper than would ever have been possible had they got it together with the poet and the soldier. They go to the brink of themselves, transported there by the animal and the night and their own passion, and for a moment they feel the beat of a full shining world in themselves, a beat whose memory will linger and make bearable the rest of their long mundane lives.

Once A Blue Moon

and cornflower cups on a silver tray
tea cooling

your mouth curled on the brim
across a small table, eyes

as hard to read, as out of reach
as books in library stacks, open

only to the initiated, to the man in the trench coat
you met on the road in the rain

his smile set on high beam. You want to remember
how the city insisted on light

lamps
in every window. Neon

burning the night through and your music
spilling its Bombay Sapphire

into the perfect hollow
between your breasts

your legs
and for the first time

the last time
the smell of him, the taste of him, the sound of his voice

even the last glimpse of him turning
even the blood on your lip

and god never seems to do anything and
you're so tired of walking down roads in the rain

in the dark
his smile still comes back to you

K.V. Skene

Moby-Dick

I never imagined that
in Arrowhead when I encouraged you to purchase
a set of engravings of the whale and Ahab that
they would end up six years later
in your airy Dublin apartment.

The one that you share with your Canadian girlfriend.

'Look,' you say when I visit awkwardly
for the first time,
'we hung the whale above the fireplace.'
You both have left the bedroom door open and I see
the other picture hangs easily over your white bed.

Life, like perverse origami, folds and twists and shapes itself
so that in your apartment, my coat lies on your crisp sheets.
I watch it from the living room,
beached upon the ivory shore,
as I sip weak tea.

And those pictures, they hang so quietly on your new walls.

Victoria Kennefick

Always the Stranger
Fiona O'Connor

He pulled up in the Octavia. We had tea and ham sandwiches then whiskey in the kitchen. Sunlight through the sycamores played over the dusty walls and everything was perfect.

'You go home now, Helena, it's enough for today.' The girl had been helping me to clean up.

'Not at all, it's fine, I'll just work away awhile.' Thinking she'd gather some bullets in the dust for her mother's armoury.

But I sent her off. She gave me the dirtiest look at the gate.

He was in great form. On his way back from the races. When the bottle was half drunk I said I'd give him a bath, if he liked.

That quietened him. He'd been doing the Irish playboy-bacchanalian routine, showing me the wad he'd won at Ballybunion, stashing it back fussily in his inside pocket. Showing me the condom he always carried too, in the same breast pocket.

'Because you never know.' He'd placed it a moment on the table, the tell-tale liver shape in blue metallic covering set there on the patterned tablecloth, between the glasses, the side plates becrumbed and mustard-smeared: a man straight out of the seventies, *Esquire* rolled up in *The Irish Field* under his arm; man with a winning horse and a condom always next to his heart.

He went to boasting then about his beekeeping and the young girlfriend pining for him in America, so beautiful and rich and yet…

The bath idea changed his mood. He wasn't sure, thought I might be joking, glancing at me from behind the banter to test my deadpan expression. The front door ajar, there was birdsong outside, occasionally a car passing up towards the Gap, but a quietness growing inside. He looked pensive, curious as well, and a bit afraid. I looked through his comedy and saw the fear beginning to gather.

The room was settling into evening's lowering, its leaf-play over the walls more like ripples on water. I ran a bath, talking to him from the lean-to bathroom. I said I'd been warming that tank all day and the water was perfect now.

When the big old tub was filled I led him in like a supplicant and removed his clothes as if they belonged to me. His skin, beyond the reddish neck and brown forearms, was blanched as almonds against jet-black body hair. His penis did not quite know what to do.

'In you get,' says I.

'What about you?' He began some pretence at unbuttoning my shirt that would of course lead to giggles then pretend exasperation before I'd do it myself. But I said, 'Who said anything about me? After three days at the races your need is greater. In you get.'

He got in, descending another level of compliance, though the first note of objection was stamping at the gate, held back because of the lure still, what you might call the sexual stakes.

I set to work washing his hair; thinning, I saw, once I'd wetted it. How vulnerable is a man's head in a woman's hands when she sees his naked scalp beneath wet hair?

The room was pleasantly steaming, mirrors foggy, slug tracings across the glass delicate evidence of their meanderings at night. Only the sounds of the taps dripping now and then and my breaths as I laboured at the lathering of his hair, as well as his own breathing not daring to let pant. He looked down along his body, faintly blue beneath the water, knowing that I looked at it too, and at his floating penis and balls in their flotsam of jet, seeing the big thigh arteries coursing blue pathways towards bald white knees poking from black hair entanglements, on down to palest feet, huge white toes emerging at the end of it all.

'You're a gorgeous man,' I told him. He laughed.

I used the blue striped jug from the kitchen to rinse the hair, set to work on his back and chest with lavender soap, lifting his arms, soaping his armpits. He fell in with my dominations, allowed me full command.

We chatted about London, where he'd been born, rehashing the early morning train pulling in to Euston from Holyhead years ago, its Irish load spilling forth, all that old stuff from the past habitual as I washed his hands, the web skin between his fingers and the same for his feet and toes. Moving then back up along his shinbones, thighs; the stomach with its river of hair to the navel and first soft warning of a paunch.

'I'll shave you now.'

'No way.'

He was in need of a good shave after three days at the races but I didn't push it.

'Stand so and I'll finish you.'

At night I watch the sky from a window in my roof. Through the sycamores: stars, clouds, clear moons, clouded moons, stars—all passages of weather, season, planetary orbit.

Moon throws silver skeletons of shape down onto the wooden floor. Sometimes I bathe myself naked in mad change spilling out of those nights, my bone-white skin against hardwood ridges, the slashed gaps of tongue in groove against my arse, touching then my own sex, my small breasts and the moon passing overhead; seeing myself reflected in the glass, a girl in the moon's eye, a moon-beamed photo of myself, seeing that, looking up at her, grimacing and crying out: 'Beam me up you dirty aul fucker, why don't you just do something instead of all the heavy silences and glidings by.' That's the kind of thing now, when I'm drunk alone and the moon is passing overhead.

'There so,' I said to him, 'stand.'

I soaped him all around his nest and under. He was looking down at my hands. I passed in beneath his scrotum, fingering his anus in passing, cradling his balls, cleaning them, then his risen prick which looked and felt unlovable somehow. It worked alright but it had a boyish, comical appearance, as though it was never really welcome on his body; as though it was always the stranger.

I cleaned it carefully. He was looking at me kindly, standing in the tub hands by his sides, shivering slightly now and again.

'All done,' I smiled. 'Clean as a whistle.'

I dried him then, gave him back his clothes.

'Cup of tea?' says I.

Holding his trousers he started to get the message. His shadowy jaw line, brown eyes, slight raise of black eyebrows—all so strange to me; there was a man I was trying to conjure him into but it wouldn't work. He wasn't him, definitely not.

He laughed. 'You're some bitch,' deadly serious beneath the laugh.

'I'll put the kettle on anyway. I could murder a cup. I'm as drunk as a pig.'

'You're a remarkable pig.'

The front door still open, we sailed through the twilight into summer's night. We drank black tea to sober ourselves then went back to whiskey from small glasses. I'd candles lit. He smoked roll-ups one after the other. His neat ritual in rolling them paced our dual pursuit: whatever that illusive capture is that two people go after on such occasions. I put on the radio. There was music; I turned it up a bit.

'Dance?'

He said no, he wouldn't. He'd prefer to just sit and watch me.

Over by the bookcase in the corner, legs crossed, one arm propped on the table, he smoked industriously; roll-up cupped as though there was a wind or something to hide. In the candlelight parts of him seemed to grow smaller, backing into shadowy impenetrable tracts of night. Other parts of him were big, more alive by contrast in the yellow flickerings: his hand with the cigarette, the glossy high forehead and nose, the tip of one polished brown boot sickled upwards towards his shin as he wagged his foot gently in time to the music.

I danced watching him watching me or bumping into furniture. I'd my shoes off. The wood was warm from my feet rubbing the same spot in the middle where I shuffled, wearing the ground out from under me.

'You're a good dancer,' he said sarcastically.

Sarah Keane came on then singing about small roads leading a person here and there. I stopped dancing to listen and by the song's end tears were running. Just the silent outriders of drunken melancholia, a few sniffles then as the mucous membranes got involved.

'Are you crying?' He announced rather than asked, leaning across to saucer the stub of his fag.

He came to me then, stood very close, his hand heavy on my shoulder.

That was enough: the little flower of pity blossomed, put forth her tearful petals. I buried my face into his tweed jacket. He, of course, drew me to him, held me tight as if I'd asked him to, like in the films.

The music was all wrong though—a set of lively reels from Ritchie Kelly's Catholic céilí boys—all jaunty accordion pip buttonings.

His jacket smelt of disappointment. I looked up to tell him, about to say, 'Your jacket smells of tobacco and something sweet and disappointed.'

He met my face, lowered to it like a horse into its bucket, started kissing.

You can see my place on the ordnance survey map. It's all about boundaries that map: small fields, threads of roads, streams, a bridge. Then a tiny matchbox shape that is mine: boundary of my domain. They use satellites for them. It looks like something on the map, my place. You can't tell it's just a bit of a hovel, a few stones piled one on another, held with mortar soft as cheese to mouse and rat, or that inside I am an anachronism, more so as the years drag on. Around it new houses gather: big fuckers, breeze-blocked fantasies all glass and show, encroaching on the small scale of my house's century and my own. You couldn't tell, either, (thankfully hidden from the satellite's blank lens) that beneath this rectangle of roof a man and a woman were beginning the old dance, linking the rattling chain.

It's not far from the ocean and across its span the satellite might show a certain shopping mall. In it a young American picks out a golfing sweater for her Irish boyfriend, although he'll never play the game—she'd be better off buying him a slow horse he could back with certainty.

I said, 'Take me from behind up against the door here.'

My front door, dilapidated portal to my domain, half-hung at best of times, open, mostly, though now closed against the black thrust of night in all its secretive antics.

He did not have to be asked twice, as they say.

Luckily he still had the tweed jacket on so that the condom was easily retrieved, unwrapped and applied to the stranger boy, now reddish—the colour of our small mountains at sunset, but sad looking actually, bidden to his master's purpose having no say in the matter, like a pious altar boy put to misdeeds below in the sacristy.

An announcer came on the radio for a sailing programme: ships and yachts and ketches, schooners and dinghies, all girl pronouns bravely voyaging. I told him to get a move on and after a good bit of fumbling and prodding he managed it somewhat and away we went.

Night was whiskey jittery, threatening hysteria. There were many things not in my mind: bees tucking into blossom, the perfect circles they trace withdrawing from a flower, entering another; the mornings to come, all of them, and my body alone in a white-painted iron bed in a white-painted room listening to trees moaning outside, their leaves lifted up by sea winds.

Nothing was in my mind but that I should spread and arch to receive a battering and should feel wood splintering my face, my hips the hard clout of another's pelvis, the budge of his prick space-shifting deeper in.

Deep down in the hold, though, nothing could fill. Deep inside: nothing. A song might touch me, or a small road leading to nowhere, no utility, but perfect in its winding; all the gradient risings and fallings away, the satin linings of trees meeting overhead, sapling and bramble entwinements, honeysuckle with blood-droplet berries against the whole spectrum of green. That road's emptiness might fill my own—if I could ever find such a road.

Up against my front door taking it: that's where all my roads delivered me. 'I hate you,' I said, resisting his thrusts, he in his tweed jacket with his trousers down around his ankles.

'I hate you, I hate you, I hate you,' my chant followed the rhythm of his pounding, my face bumping in time against the doorframe. I could smell its sour, smoky odour, taste dirt. He was working away still, like he had his head in a different room, his hind quarters left behind in the stables.

'I fucking hate you, fucking, fucking, fucking hate you.'

The roads tilting, roads hitting me, a car crash never finding any cease in the deadly occasioning of his poor altar boy responsorial thrusts—man of tweed and bees, Golden Virginia and bookies' squanderings.

'I HATE YOU, YOU FUCKER.'

He stopped. He withdrew. He stooped to deal with the altar boy. Bewildered, he pulled up his trousers.

I was in a heap then, weeping. 'Here,' he put a glass to my mouth. I swallowed the burn of a small mouthful. Here in this hot little house of the threadworm road he'd his head bowed trying to figure this one out. The candlelight was licking out of deep wells of molten wax throwing shadows of elongated pitch. Spiders reversed back into crevices as he sat back down, as his shadow too sat back down in his old place in the corner.

An Oscar Peterson number came on. I said I was sorry then.

He said it was all right and not to worry.

I said sorry again anyway.

He poured himself the last of the whiskey, one hand in his trouser pocket. He sat looking at the glass on the table as though it gave grounds for serious concern.

'It wasn't you,' I said, 'I was… you know..?'

He nodded.

I was breathing these big, sobbing, exhausted catch-breaths, faintly pleasurable because numb: everything feeling sodden and cleaned out after the riots.

I said I'd some problems with sex.

He looked up from the jewel gleaming in his glass.

I shrugged. A clock on the bookshelf behind his head ticked. On its face was a girl in a pink bonnet with a little pet duck that waddled side to side with meticulous timing.

'It's getting very late,' I smiled.

'Mmm.' He picked up his tobacco as though to go. I noticed tufts of black hair on the backs of his hands.

I thought for an instant about Helena, the girl I'd sent home earlier; she was asleep in her bed no doubt, at this time of night.

'Not too late for your girl in America though—she'll only be waking up just. And thinking of you, no doubt.'

One of the candles snuffed out; the other wicks were burning angrily from puddles of wax in the table. Black-lettered titles on the books behind him bid to distract my attention with ridiculous information.

He started another roll-up, taking deep breaths, sighing on the exhalations, almost groans they sounded. He was like a cross parent deciding on the next course of action with some wearying offspring.

'I'm going to tell you something,' he whispered, 'but it's a secret. I've never told it to anyone, never.' He looked at me. 'You'll be the first.'

I nodded, gave him the small brave smile to show I understood.

'You'll turn off the radio now please,' he says, so I did. I pulled a cardigan around me, cold after the hysteria, and sat back down opposite him like the good girl I had become.

'I was in prison once.' He let the words settle in the quiet.

'God, I'd never have thought that now, wouldn't have figured it.'

'Over in England,' he said.

My little black and white cat came in from the bedroom as though to hear the worst.

She arched herself by his legs; he leaned to stroke her.

'For long?'

'Mmm.'

'Really?'

He picked up the cat, doting her a while. She gave way to a low purring drone. He'd his feet turned in towards each other, sitting so as to contain the cat comfortably in his lap, dappling her snow-white throat.

'I murdered someone,' he told her, looking into her eyes kindly, then at me too.

'You did not,' I blurted.

'Eight years in British jails then they let me out to come home. Oh, yes,' he told the cat, drawing up her head further, elongating her neck and fondling her to her delight.

Another candle gave up the ghost; I thought of switching on a light but couldn't yet.

'Self defence,' he announced as though she'd asked him why.

'Fella came up behind me. Coming out of a station one night—Walt-ham-stow, do you know that place?' He'd her head cupped in his hand, pulled her up to meet his nose.

'No one around. He comes from behind. Hits me hard, hits my head, back of my head,' he felt the back of his skull, 'with a hammer.'

'Jesus Christ.'

'I killed him then.'

He stretched out his hands, examining the long fingers, curved thumbs, the pale, smooth palms, turning them round slowly as though they were in a display case. The cat seemed fascinated by them too.

'I was trained, you see, in the army. My hands, I've a black belt. I was trained and something kicked in.' He was silent for ages. The cat started to clean herself and I was glad to watch her.

'I caught hold of him, brought him down...'

I gave a little start.

'... my own blood dripping onto him. I didn't shed a drop of his. Only me that bled.'

Holding the cat close to his chest with his two hands so that she looked out from his body, from his tweed jacket, they both looked at me.

'There's a place in your neck,' he used the cat to demonstrate, 'a pressure point. If you know it you can kill anything. You just put a little pressure on.' The cat yowled, trying to pull away. 'It doesn't take long actually. No force, only you have to know exactly where to squeeze.'

The cat was silent, her legs treading frantically, her eyes tight closed.

'It's the know-how, you see? Isn't that it kitty, nice little kitty.' He was looking hard at me, then he let her go and she shot away with an angry snarl and a cry of pain.

I got up all shaky, made for the door, far away and hard to get open. When I'd managed it the night came right up to me. When I opened the rickety slow door the night was waiting there, soot black, stifling.

I fell over groping for the sweeping brush.

'You get out now.' Bellowing from the floor I held up the brush as though I'd the winning ticket, and crawled out into pitch black, into the terrible anticipation of the night.

'Get the fuck out of my house now, you.' What else could I do but shout? I was ready to run but there was no point in that.

'BASTARD,' I roared.

When he did come out, dipping his head at the low sash, I held up the brush again, cowering back as he passed close.

'Know where to press,' he says.

He walked away and I was left there in the darkness missing him.

FEATURED POET

TADHG RUSSELL lives in Doneraile, North Cork, and has been writing poetry for the last number of years. One of Tadhg's poems took second place in the 2011 Gregory O'Donoghue International Poetry Competition; he was also shortlisted for the Patrick Kavanagh Award in 2010. His work has been published by *West 47*, *Cyphers*, *Southword*, *The Stony Thursday Book*, *The Sunday Tribune* and *The Stinging Fly*. His short stories have appeared in Cork's *Evening Echo* newspaper.

The Whole Shebang

The all night drunk presses his purpled face
against the window of a still closed café,
its tables stacked with chairs, the postman
gives him a wide berth and posts a letter
—wrong name, right address—through a brass slip,
a motorist catches his reflection in a shop display,
the whole shebang backlit by sunrise, some dogs
decide to meet, same time same place, next week,
the undiscovered body in an alley lets a hand slap
against the side of a skip, startling the silence, doors
unlock here and there, this is the day yesterday
promised, a robin tries out a new tune, the notes
falling on deaf ears, shadows run ahead like unleashed
pets, from a satellite the street appears no different
than a million others, as the lens zooms back,
and again the planet turns bluegreen like an open eye.

Wave

Children explode through school gates in a swarm
of blue, a surging wave that breaks between cars
held to attention in swirling, shriekish air,
an enthusiasm that evaporates in every direction,
until the stray dog is stray again, and shadows
realign themselves with falling silence, twilight,
a scatter of leaves, blown first one way, then another.

The Watchman

A green surge has overtaken the earthmover's work,
weeds and grass mottle the unfinished roadways,
already some windows are boarded over, at night
it appears like a set from an abandoned disaster film,
dogs stray and nose around, the wind plays cards
with shadows, too young for ghosts the watchman points
his torch like a light sabre through empty rooms,
remembers days in the sun, bare-chested, counting
the number of blocks lain. There is no one to blame.
He waves at a passing car in the darkness, smokes
a cigarette, wonders where anybody could be going at this
time of night, kicks a pebble into the black. Later it rains.

The Question

He asks if there are fish on the moon, waits
for a reply, then turns back toward the window,
we are mid-Atlantic going in the wrong direction,
it's the middle of the night, so people are sleeping,
lights turned down low, engines pulsing a single
hummed note, someone coughs, a drowsy, soft
bell rings, the stewardess moves between mulled rows,
even her footfalls sound muffled, again the question,
his mother leans forward, says something I can't
quite hear, the plane banks, just enough to show
a distant sunrise on the far horizon, each porthole
a momentary blaze of gold, at journey's end
we will disperse like a shoal frightened of new light,
all save one, who closes his eyes, begins to dream.

The Situation

Alcohol speaks in a low voice, swears this
won't happen again, will say anything to make
the listener believe, up to and including fooling
itself, telling anyone within earshot what it
thinks they want to hear, it goes on like this
for a long while, almost pleading, hoping someone
might feel sorry, feel pity, not betrayal or disgust, no,
but there's something else, some other voice, more
human, some part that isn't dead yet, alcohol turns
round quickly and sneers in its direction, its clear
how this will play out, morning sun enters the room,
making shadows, a telephone rings, the situation continues
in this direction, until it can't possibly go any further.

Tadhg Russell

Downturn

Against rain, these dry days make no demand,
and settle between themselves a long lost argument.
We have been here before and know the feeling well,
so cloud-shadows make no difference, obscure no reality,
we look to the east in hopes of thunder, to the west it stays
schtum, instead silence gathers, an arid breeze points a finger,
but direction itself means nothing now, even if we realise
it means something else, the dust blames bad planning, a shortage
of outcome, at night people watch the weather forecast,
given in sign, keep an eye out for the next drop.

Interpretation

Fields away, they recognised the sound for what
it was, others took note of the time, as much
to convince themselves as anybody else, people
put down their work to listen, and if you asked
each of them to describe what they heard, a hundred
various images might crowd your mind, in time
rumour gave the story a life of its own, even when they
remembered, if at all, men and women would gaze
towards the middle distance and smile, while others
would put their hands to their ears, close their eyes.

Tadhg Russell

The Rest of the Day

A stranger pulled into the drive around noon
wanting to know about a family I had never
heard of, had they lived here once, sunshine
warmed my back as I leaned in at the passenger's
window, answering his question, he didn't seem
disappointed, but there was a look to his eyes,
a car went by on the road outside and after
a little silence, he began to speak, words marking
time in a measured, low tone, each sentence
building a picture of a life lived, he didn't
seem embarrassed, just happy to be talking
to someone else, someone he had never met before
and probably never would again, how he had spent
years in jail, his sons and daughters
scattered across the globe, his wife indifferent,
bad health following bad luck, even so, he wasn't
bitter, no, he felt fortunate, privileged you might say
as he went on in this pattern for another while,
me listening, moving from one foot to another,
and when he was gone, standing alone again,
wondering what I would do with the rest of the day.

Tadhg Russell

Now

A day wide open to possibility, the world
held at bay, the phone off the hook, the television
unplugged, the newspaper left in a roll
on the kitchen table; he worked all morning
in the garden under bright sunlight tempered
by a cooling breeze, fell into a rhythm
with the earth, the past and future standing
back, around about noon he rose up
and stretched tired muscles, it was then
he heard somebody call his name, looking
to see where the voice was coming from
he shaded his eyes with one hand, nobody,
again the voice, was he going crazy? He laughed
to himself, but searched anyway; inside the house
he smoked a cigarette, sat at the table, got up,
unable to settle, the sky was still blue, the sun
shining, no mystery in that, and if he wanted
he could leave this place forever, what would
it matter, nobody counts that much, this life he thought,
means one thing to many, everything to a few.

Tadhg Russell

Return
David Hayden

On my last day, the day that is upon me, the big lady with the flowery apron will arrive and bustle about, preparing the room, making every surface shine white. She will leave without talking to me. I will never know her name. She will never speak mine.

Edith.

I will lie comfortably on the bed in my nightdress, as I do today, looking at the cannula in my hand; smaller than I was, as small as I once was. Summer will reach me from the courtyard through the window's narrow opening on the slow moving scent of the gum trees.

Out of the inner dark they begin to show themselves.

Daddy is wearing his long black overcoat and stands turning his hat in his hands. Mummy's perfume arrives next, tea rose, and then I see her in a yellow summer dress, her hair pinned up in loose rolls. She moves forward and the bag that she holds crackles. Daddy takes the loop handles and begins to remove small parcels neatly wrapped in shiny gold and brick red paper.

'For later,' he says.

Mummy hugs me, presses me, speaking close to my ear so that I cannot understand her.

'You've been gone such a long time,' is all I can say at first.

'Where did you go?'

Mummy stands back from me.

'We've missed you too.'

She sits on the bed and smoothes down the coverlet.

They become still, so quiet that I think they might go away again.

Then Daddy speaks.

'Don't you remember? Mummy and I took the train from Victoria to Dover Marine and caught the ferry. We were going to France. We rented a car in Calais and made for Paris. The hotel was seedy but charming. The perfect place. We went dancing; the floor was so small that we filled it on our own. I don't think I've ever felt so close to your mother as on our last evening in Paris.'

The colour leaves Mummy's face, her features fade away; her large brown eyes gaze into mine.

'We began to drive south heading for an appointment with an agent at Toulouse to discuss properties in the Lot Valley. We had received advance details about a number of places and your mother and I were particularly keen to look at an old mill house near a village called Vayrac. There was a small cottage with several large buildings with potential for conversion, a generous stand of walnut trees and, as one might expect, a tributary of the Lot river running through the grounds. The surrounding area, we knew, was beautiful and, as yet, unspoiled by people like us grubbing around for rural idylls. I was sure that we would spend many happy summers there.'

Daddy reaches into his coat but finding nothing he withdraws his hand and pats his chest at the empty pocket.

'I was driving down a long poplar-lined road when I noticed the sky changing colour and a hissing began that I thought for a second was the radiator overheating, but which, I soon realised, was a fine orange dust skittering over the windscreen. I could feel the wind pick up behind us, and the hiss turned to a gush and the wheels' revolutions began to soften. The fields, the farms, the fences began to blur and sink and the trees sagged under their colourful burden. The air in the car remained cool and fresh but the world outside grew wilder and redder. Eventually we could see nothing through any window and I had to accept that we were no longer moving.

'The steady patter of falling dust soothed and lulled us, and your mother and I fell asleep, separating into our dreams. On waking we found that we were buried, the car packed in a warm mass of fine desiccants. Your mother turned on the overhead light and I rummaged in the glove compartment for something to eat, though neither of us was hungry. I found a travellers' tin of boiled sweets. I suggested that we talk about something, Paris or you, and your mother said…'

'I believe this is a marvellous opportunity for us *not* to speak, Darling.'

'Admirable woman. So we sat and listened to the slight shiftings of the dust, breathed the dry air and waited. I ventured that it might be a good idea if we were to turn the light out to conserve the battery but your mother said…'

'I can't see what difference that will make. We're not going any farther.'

'Yes. You see, it didn't matter. I had a hip flask filled with a good, single whiskey, which I've always preferred to malt, and we dined on that and boiled sweets whenever the desire came on; which wasn't often. Nature didn't impose any further inconveniences on us and I began to be aware of how very tired I had become, and when I was certain that I was free, I submitted to a feeling of blissful release that I had never before experienced, and I slept and slept.'

'So very tired,' says Mummy.

'We were woken by a rushing, collapsing sound. Straight ridges were appearing in the matter pressed against the windows, visible by the yellow light that still flickered above. The wind had risen and was, in turn, raising our car out of its sandy captivity. The air grew frantic all around us and the particles lifted and flew, who knows where.'

'Heavenwards,' says Mummy, her mouth twisting but not smiling.

'I started the car and we continued on our way to Toulouse but when we reached the agent's offices we found that they were closed. It was then that we turned around and came back home. I'm sorry that we missed so much. There was nothing that we could do, Darling.'

Daddy takes out his pipe and sucks a few times to check the air flow before getting a floppy leather pouch from which he brings out rough pinches of tobacco that he pushes into the pipe's bowl. His teeth click on the stem as he focuses on the crossed red circle of a sign that reads 'No Smoking.' Daddy slips the pipe into the side pocket of his overcoat. I turn my head with some difficulty and I smile at him and he grins back like a naughty boy.

'What happened was more like this, Sweetie,' starts Mummy.

'We ran for the balloon which was rocking in the wind, despite the guy ropes, as if it were being pulled by an invisible hand. The rain lashed down. I was so glad that I was wearing the sou'wester that your father bought me. The mud was sucking at my boots and slowing me down. Your father pulled me by the hand and I nearly fell over but we reached the basket and clambered inside before, with one enormous heave, the balloon leaped off the ground and lunged for the sky leaving the pilot—or whatever they're called—waving on the ground. I did feel sorry for the fellow.

'The sky grew bigger and bigger as we fell towards the clouds that tossed icy rain onto us, and then suddenly we broke through, still rising, out into brilliant sunshine. I can't tell you how marvellous it was to be bathed in that warm, buttery light. But before long the sky grew paler and weaker, turning white then darkening blue before we came up into the outer blackness where the stars shone all about like… like nothing but stars. It wasn't nearly as cold as you might imagine and we continued to fall towards the moon.

'We landed softly enough but in a tangle so that it took us a while to crawl out. We had the place to ourselves. At first I thought that everything looked the same, but once my eyes became accustomed to the conditions I began to discern, in the seeming uniformity, a captivating variety of form. Your father and I went for long walks, there wasn't a whisper of air and the land was easy under foot. We camped under the basket on a tartan rug, which was adequately comfortable, and time passed in that manner.

'One morning we were standing facing home when a light breeze rose up and began to play around us. Your father realised what was happening sooner than I and began to untangle the ropes and set the basket straight, and by the time the gale was truly up we were crouching inside, braced for the ascent. The balloon re-inflated like a great red lung and pulled us back to Earth. The air gyred as we plunged into the atmosphere and I lost my emerald cloche hat; a favourite of mine, such a pity. The storm abated, the balloon floated down pacifically and we debouched onto the strand. Your father and I were ravenously hungry so we walked up to the old hotel and ate breakfast; kedgeree and everything. I can't tell you how delightful it was. Then we walked home and here you are, my darling. Home without us. Waiting.'

Mummy never cries so I am shocked when I see her open her clutch purse, take out a perfect white square of linen and dab her eyes and cheeks. Daddy puts his arm around her and kisses Mummy once on the ear. She stops sobbing and returns the handkerchief to its proper place and Daddy talks.

'What your mother meant was that we were at Dotty's summer house party…'

'She does so hate it when you call her Dotty,' says Mummy.

'… and we were all gathered in the sitting room after the outlying guests had gone home and Victor suggested that we play hunt the trophy. Now Dorothy and Victor had set up all the clues beforehand as a special treat so we didn't want to be spoilsports but we did insist, against bitter opposition, that your mother and I would not be split asunder. We took our sheaf of clues and our brandies and set off into the house. We bumped into Gerald and Sylvia in the kitchen, which I understand wasn't supposed to happen, and, of course, Gerry started to moo on about his printing business so we fled to the library where we quickly gathered our wits.

'The theme was fairy tales with each clue taken from a different colour of those marvellous books that, as luck would have it, my mother used to own, and which I had read backwards and forwards before I knew that they weren't for boys.'

Mummy looks as if she might cough.

'Of course, your mother knows the books too. So the upshot was that we romped through the trail, the yellow dwarf, the troll's daughter, Drakestail, the glass axe and so on, until we came to the last clue which came from The Silver Fairy. This was the story of the Sunken Princess who is betrothed by her wicked guardian to a handsome prince who lives in a moss-covered castle deep in the Broken Mountains. The princess travels alone through the swaying trees of a misty forest, her wedding dress shining white, scattered with perfect pearls that glitter like a scattering of tiny tears. The brave girl climbs up the slippery slate ramp and into the castle, her breath curling white through the air and rising away into the darkness. She mounts the steps that spiral up to join a long corridor that leads to another corridor that leads to the icy, airless room that is her bridal chamber.

'The girl approaches. Before her is a vast bed dressed in mildewed yellow satin, surrounded by flickering candles resting in shivering bowls of water, their surfaces starting to crisp over with ice. She sits on the bed then swings her legs up and reclines on the mattress, her chestnut hair fanning over the pillow. The handsome prince enters through a hidden panelled door and as he walks towards her his grey livery falls away, his skin and flesh slop to the floor revealing the livid form of her guardian. The princess looks around for anyone, anything to rescue her but there is no one. 'Room, help me!' she cries, but the room cannot help her. 'Candles, help me!' she cries, but the candles cannot help her. 'Bed, help me!' she cries and the bed begins to ripple and soften, the mattress rises slightly before sinking down, down into the world through the roots of the mountain, down and out and up into a bright orange world and out of the story. The wicked guardian jumps onto the sunken bed and falls down and down and is caught in the fiery heat at the centre of the world where he burns still.'

Daddy coughs and runs his hand through his shining hair.

'So after searching into the dimmest recesses of the house your mother and I finally found a musty bedroom with a four-poster bed, hung around with moth-eaten drapes. We searched for some time but couldn't find the answer and then your mother, the clever thing, suggested that we try the bed. We lay down on the dusty covers, and high over us pinned to the canopy was the answer; must've used a stepladder. I'm sorry to say but we'd had the best part of a bottle of wine each, Darling, and the brandy must have finished us off, because we fell into the deepest sleep, and when we woke up I remember a delicious smell of toasted cinnamon and an unaccountable soft warmth under my back. We sat up and saw the old house fallen, scorched and broken down all around us, and your mother and I lying on a bed of ash without a scratch on us. There wasn't a soul in the grounds and only our car was left of all the partygoers'. I immediately started her up and we came home to you as quickly as we could.'

Mummy turns from Daddy and presses my knee gently; she smiles slowly, her eyes glittering, the colour rising on her cheeks, her face radiant, limitless. I can see the shape and meaning of the whole world hovering over me; loving me. Daddy puts his hat on and takes it off again. I look down at my hands withered and veiny, small and smooth and pink.

'Darling, I would have thought that you'd remember what happened,' said Mummy. 'It had been a dreadful winter and we'd all been stuck inside far too much for our own good and we'd managed to clamber up to March, but instead of the first feeble rays of the blessed dawn of life reaching down to warm our clammy bones, all that came was rain. Torrents, sheets, buckets and bathtubs of icy, dreary rain. Then one Sunday your father put down his pipe, stood up and said…'

'Are we not men? To cower thus squinting under a few pale drops of water. Let us go forth,' says Daddy.

'Magnificent, Darling,' says Mummy. 'So we rugged up and ventured out into the wind-bent world and struggled up to the park. Umbrellas were useless and despite our best efforts we were all soaked to a mush. We made for the Pavilion, squelched in and ordered tea and buns from the poor soul whose office it was to provide for waifs like ourselves. I can't tell you but that it was the most delicious tea I've ever tasted and we felt fortified, emboldened even, to take you outside and attempt some proper fun. Daddy and I brought you to the boating lake, unsurprisingly there was no attendant in view, so we took matters into our own hands and located the most stable looking vessel and your father and I climbed in. One of us must have knocked the bank with an oar because we started to pull away from the shore and by the time we had fitted the oars into the rowlocks we had drifted quite a distance from you. I saw you waving, my angel, and it broke my heart, but no matter how hard we rowed the boat kept moving further away. There was water stretching to every horizon and the only dry land in sight was the bank where you stood and the path that led up to the Pavilion. A current had gripped the boat and was dragging us towards the lowering sky. Your father had had the foresight to bring a bag of toffee bonbons with him so we didn't starve.

'The rain stopped eventually but the water took a long time to fall away. When the flood subsided we found ourselves forked high in the top of a tree. The leaves were fat and glossy, and purple fruit hung in clusters close to hand but we didn't trust them, Darling. We climbed down through knotted boughs and branches, past founts of mistletoe and nests filled with spoons and medals and pocket watches, before shinning down the trunk onto the path. We were immediately jostled by a group of schoolboys in blue jerseys running towards a playing field but in doing so they had turned us in the right direction for home. We walked on and here we are.'

'Here we are,' says Daddy.

The clock ticks with a *suck-suck, suck-suck* and the light dims outside and I close my eyes and remember the day that I stood in the parlour, still and cold, my uncle telling me that they were never coming home. And I open my eyes and they stand there smiling, smiling, and the night will come on and the moon will come out and traverse the sky and the dawn will return and we will stand there together smiling, smiling.

Return

the court of the red queen

She came on the spur of the moment, and the hollow dreamers and politicians all find subtle reasons for that, slender enough to pass between the earth and moon. We feel like metaphysical wallflowers hovering around the perimeter of the ballroom hoping something or other will ask us to dance. Her spies are everywhere. Inflation is rampant. The silhouettes of antiquity will abruptly emerge from over the horizon like the sudden flash of a truck's headlights in the night. Jack and Jill went up the hill. Where are they now?

Joe Dresner

dream for sale

The mountains ignore us studiously. The rivers pretend to have forgotten our names. We had keys as thick and ornate as slices of cake for stolen mansions which we passed from generation to generation until they were lost. The argument jackknifes in the fields and we find ourselves haranguing an increasingly bored auditorium. There are at least five minutes left of this cold democracy.

Joe Dresner

The Lost Notebook

1.

Fair enough, we brought them
    to the Rodin Museum
        to visit the Gates of Hell,

so they invited us to the catacombs,
    a place we'd never thought of touring,
        but who better to lead us

past the sign proclaiming, *Stop,*
    You are Entering the Empire
        of Death! than our grown children?

2.

Almost alone among the six million
    anonymous dead, the quarryman
        Francois Décure is remembered,

and not for how he performed his day job,
    or how he cared for his wife
        or any offspring he may have had,

but for what he did in the mines
    on his lunch breaks,
        which was to chip away at memory

and carve a limestone tableau
    of a Minorcan fortress, recreating the view
        from his former prison window:

parapets and towers, bridges, stairs
    and ramparts still bloom like a night garden
        beneath the streets of Paris.

3.

Soldier, prisoner, quarryman—
        almost nothing in his life resembles mine,
                except for all those lunch breaks

I took on night shift decades ago,
        climbing out a fourth floor window
                onto the slanting hospital roof

where I could perch against a gable
        and write. All that summer
                I filled a notebook—nighthawks

harrowed the air, the Cumberlands
        slept uneasily in the east,
                my wife and children

in the apartment across the road
        floated above their beds,
                and beneath me

in the hospital, someone
        was setting off to the realm
                of the dead, someone else

was arriving amidst obscenities
        and pleas, and having only
                a half hour each night,

I scribbled as fast as I could,
        I tried to get everything down.
                And failed, of course,

and then lost even that—
        as my wife's granny said
                Three moves are as good as a fire.

I have only the memory of opening
        a window and stooping through it,
                of walking the heights

to my favorite spot, then starting to write
        as silent hospital shoes braced
                myself against the sloping roof.

Ted Deppe

Transition
Gina Moxley

His mother's ankles were like puff balls from the flight, her sandal straps embedded in billows of wintery flesh. She had booked in for a spray tan before they left but his father had misread the travel arrangements so she had to come in her original colour: Irish white. She was not happy. His father had steadily sipped beer since they left Dublin: half a day away. His hangover was just kicking in. He wasn't happy either. They hardly ever spoke to each other, and if they did it followed an inevitable pattern, with either taking the lead:
    'Don't start.'
    'Don't you start.'
    'Oh, here we go.'
    He and his father hadn't spoken for weeks. In jetlagged silence Ronan watched his parents drag their suitcases up the two flights of concrete stairs—bumb bumb bumb. It was seven in the morning and already thirty-two degrees. They'd been travelling all night. Nobody had bothered to show them up to their accommodation. Once the padlock—no handle, just a padlock—had been undone, their door opened into a very basic bedroom: a double and single bed, a wardrobe, a table ringed where drinks had once been, two plastic chairs and a cracked mirror. Three threadbare towels had been twisted into a shape on the bed. It may have been a palm tree. Ronan began to panic. Even though he was sure his parents didn't have sex anymore—he'd heard his mother on the phone to her sister say, 'I'd leave him if I had the money,'—there was no way he was going to sleep in the same room as them. Not a chance.
    He let his backpack drop and loped around the rest of the apartment; he was sixteen and all limbs. Peering into the dark bathroom he noticed only ants. He closed the door quickly before his mother saw in. Next to it was a long, narrow room with an industrial type sink, a small fridge and a very small window, way up high, out of reach. Stifling. A kitchen but for a cooker. But space enough for the single bed. No door but at least he wouldn't be in the same room as them. Yep, that would do. He kicked off his runners:

they stank, and peeled off his socks. He had lambs' brains for feet.

'It's like a flat in Galway or something,' his mother said, as she deflated like a soufflé on one of her suitcases. Ronan had never been inside a flat in Galway nor had any of them been to India before but he sort of knew what she meant. It was unlike any place they'd ever stayed in before, was what she was saying. Holidays were her chance to be more upmarket than she was at home. This would not do.

'A kip,' she spat.

Ronan was warming to its studenty functionalism and had an idea that maybe he'd move to Galway when he finished school—if he finished school—to do a course or something. Yeah. Or even get a job. He was in his transition year, he was meant to be thinking about what to do when he left. That's if he wasn't suspended first. One more strike and he was out. He'd been warned twice already this term, first time for smoking—he'd since given up—and then for calling the soccer coach an asshole. Starlings were nesting in a broken floodlight at the pitch and perfectly imitated the ref's whistle. All the guys knew the difference between the birds and the ref, any fool would, but the new coach didn't and tore into Ronan for not obeying the referee's call. Ronan didn't bother to explain, just shook his head and smirked, 'Asshole'. The way he saw it, the coach was the one on probation. The team needed him, soccer was the one thing he excelled at, but he didn't know whether he'd bother going back. Probably not. So, he could smoke again with impunity. There, he nodded to himself that was the thinking done, his future was sorted, he was going to move into a kip in Galway.

His father, an electrician, flicked a switch near the door and the enormous fan over the bed juddered to life, rotating in a buckled circle before speeding up to a blur. It sounded as if there was an aircraft in the room. Ronan and his father stepped back and stared up at it, expecting the ceiling to take off, while his mother put her head in her hands. His father jabbed at the switch; the fan slowly flapped to a halt. Assuming his parents would take the renewed silence as a signal to flare up—it was only a matter of time—Ronan stepped out onto the balcony. Bare concrete draped in some plant, plastic chairs and a rickety table. Beyond, the world was lurid, electrified, hissing with insects, sprinklers, unfamiliar smells, a boom box of birdsong. He overlooked a group of squealing, barefoot kids carrying each other around a scrubby yard. No adults were in evidence. The kids waved and shouted, 'Hello, hello,' when they saw him and ran at the dividing fence. One of the them plucked some iridescent red flowers: huge blooms in the process of turning themselves inside out, revealing a bobbing proboscis at their centre. Offering them up to him, she said, 'Welcome. My brother. My friend.' She had a harelip. Their blatant friendliness embarrassed him. He didn't know how to react to such openness. He felt moved but didn't recognise it as such, it wasn't a feeling he was that familiar with. He half waved back. Then, a man in a washed out military uniform, complete with beret and gun, an Indian Che Guevara, stepped out from the shadow of the balcony beneath, looked up and said something that sounded like 'Nice day.' Ronan, feeling like a king, leant over his security man and subjects and said, 'Yeah, for Galway.' He returned to the bedroom and dragged the single bed into the skinny room as his mother undid the first of her suitcases and unpacked her make-up bag which was wedged between layers of new clothes bought on credit. She took out her eyebrow tweezers and did what she always did in testing situations: she began to pluck the disappointment from her frown. His father stood in the middle of the room at a loss.

While his parents slept off their jetlag Ronan went to change some money into rupees. It was meant to be cheap here; he figured fifty euro should keep him going until he saw something he wanted to buy. On Saturdays he washed cars at the local garage, it was a handy number, he doubled his wages in tips. He emerged with a wedge of notes, fat as an airport novel, held together by a crude copper staple, wrapped in newspaper. He had no idea what it was worth here but he felt inordinately rich. This is what it must be like being a bank robber or politician, he thought, this unearned wealth. Fluttery with excess, he sat by the pool and ordered a coke. No ice. He wished he could think of something more extravagant. The waiter brought him a tray with eggs, toast and flowers; it was included in the package.

'Welcome.'

The other guests having breakfast were predominantly fat, old and English. He resented them for making him feel less intrepid. What was the big deal about India if even grannies came all that way? And where were the hippies and stoners? Probably asleep half the day. No one was younger than ancient. A single child, he was used to being on his own but wondered how his mother would fare. She made friends easily on holiday; within minutes she'd be sitting on a lounger with a woman she'd never seen before in her life, swapping secrets and sun cream while his father lay in the sun and baked. That was what did it for her, chatting to strangers and dressing up. And his dad? It wasn't so much that he zoned out, he was as good as not there. This would probably be his last holiday with them anyway.

Plastic chairs scraped beside him. A granny said, 'Sit down.'

'Can't drink me facking tea can Oi?' a tattooed geezer with smudged glasses whined. He was thrusting a cup and jug at the waiter. Liquid slopped onto the waiter's shoe.

'Facking milk's hot again, innit? Told yeh yesterday, diddin Oi? Oi wannit cold.'

The waiter remained serene. 'Hot drink, hot milk,' he replied with unimpeachable logic. When he spoke it sounded as if he was gargling simultaneously, a lovely gurgly sound. Accepting the cup and jug onto his tray, he waggled his head in a figure of eight and retreated. Now that was a good answer Ronan felt, nodding the waiter his due. Difficult to argue with that. Asshole seemed weak.

An elderly man, edging the grass with a scissors, looked at Ronan as if they were in a reciprocal zoo, and said the 'Nice day' thing. Was that it? Nice day? Why would they need to say nice day here when every day was nice. Surely, only people who lived in miserable climates needed to comment on it. 'Can you believe it? Nice day.' No, that wasn't it; there was an 'm' in there somewhere. And possibly an 's'. Ronan figured it meant hello and said, 'Hey.' The man was tiny, dressed only in a loincloth. His body didn't have a scrap of fat, just sinews, muscle and bone. He unwound the fabric from around his head and wiped his sweaty face. Little walnut head on him, he was eighty if he was a day. Ronan slipped his hand into the newspaper package on his lap and detached the top note. He had a moment of panic—what if it's worth only about two cent? So he pulled a note from the underside of the bundle, figuring they would be of a higher denomination, scrunched the two together and passed them to the old man. Secreting the cash into his waistband, the man bowed his head graciously and continued bowing until he was on the ground again, back at work, snipping away. Ronan sat back. King one minute, Robin Hood the next. He had never given money to anybody before and had no idea what had prompted his largesse. It wasn't like the guy was begging or anything. He looked down at the man whose feet were as knobbled and taut as fresh ginger, and felt great.

At the opposite end of the pool, a tawny girl stepped out of her halter neck dress, took a deep breath and dived into the water. Her bikini was the same tone as her skin. She swam the length along the bottom, a gold filament, darting from side to side. Ronan played the camera game with himself, where he blinked like a shutter, recording images, no analysis, just lodge and store, for editing at some later date. He thought she smiled at him when she came up for air. Blink. She did a flip, light bouncing off her barely covered bottom. Blink. His skin tightened. Each time she swam towards him he implored her to look at him. Blink. Please. She did ten lengths in ten breaths—his eyes followed every stroke—and then hopped out. A pool boy offered a towel, she said something touching his arm, and he smiled shyly. She put her dress on over her wet bikini and disappeared. Her neck, her neck, her neck. Blink. Blink. Blink. Longing hurt his chest. Hiding his hard on with his money Ronan went off to lie down.

'Stand back, they buck,' Ronan's dad said, declaring an emergency and physically barring his wife's path. Their guidebook had warned of unpredictable wildlife. Sure enough, here they were. The goats reversed into each other, tottering on their hooves, clearing the track. A slow procession of women in saris carrying baskets on their heads climbed a vertical catwalk of bamboo scaffolding on the building site beside them. Children making bricks didn't give them a glance. Predictably, the goats ate whatever was handy. Parents, thought Ronan, what doesn't shock them, frightens them. They were halfway already, and he decided to risk it and lead the way. And when they got to it, the beach stretched on to forever, palm trees, massive waves, thundering foam. They stood there, the gangly teenager and his white parents, in awe. His mother visibly thawed. It was so blindingly beautiful not one of them could think of a thing to say. The spectacle was too big for them. They picked their way across scorching sand to a shack and sat in the shade. Each scrutinised the menu; they often had Indian take outs at home so they weren't afraid.

'Look, Ro,' Ronan's father said, forgetting that he hadn't spoken to his son since the asshole incident. A whiff of entente. 'Cauliflower with cheese saucers.'

Giggles erupted from each of them.

'Number twenty one,' his mum said.

The men scanned their menus. 21. Leg of Lamp. And howled. He couldn't remember when last he'd laughed like that with his parents. If ever. It was like they were stoned. Convulsing, he had to put the menu away and ordered what he thought was a smoothie. A mango lassi arrived. They each took a sip. His mother winced.

'Smells like…oh Jesus, the inside of a rubber glove.'

And they were off again, hysterical, ridding themselves of the greyness and dampness of home.

An arm ending in a stump placed a tattered card on their table. It declared the carrier of the card to be a leper. Officially. They looked at the biblical creature that had placed it. Bearded and upright, he exposed a running sore on his leg. Ronan's mother shook her head and said, 'No thanks.' His father put some money on the table. They averted their eyes as the man picked it up. He bowed in thanks and moved on. A hot breeze shuffled the palm frond roof. The ocean rolled to and fro. So much blue. Ronan stared out at the uninterrupted horizon and wondered how people ever thought the earth was flat. There was clearly a curve.

'He looked like Saint Patrick,' his mother said, feebly breaking their silence.

'A bit,' his father conceded and called for the bill. Ronan stopped him, saying, 'I'll get it.' His father looked at him in amazement. Ronan always let them pay. But here, here was different. He was loaded.

'Wey hey,' he shrugged and waved away the change.

'Right, back to the pool for me,' his mum said. 'That's enough unpredictable wildlife for one day.'

Diving quickly under the wave just before it broke, Ronan somersaulted underwater on the edge of panic, the violence and scramble of the swirl surprised him, and he thought he might drown. Surrender, he told himself. Surrender to its force. He rotated in the murk, with no sense of which end was up. The wave broke, sunlight through the water, and it spewed him back out. Breathless, he was stunned to have survived it. Other seas he's swum in weren't half as rough. Second time he tried, he grazed his forehead off the bottom. The tide dragged him down the beach away from the tourists. It was the best water, the best beach, he felt unbelievably alive. He kept doing it over and over, not caring where he ended up. A massive roller came towards him, and under he went. In the underwater chaos he crashed into one body, then another, wriggling elvers, teenagers like himself. They surfaced, startled. He was encircled by a group of boys around his own age, shy that they'd snared a tourist.

'Namaste,' one of the Indian boys said.

The others stood waist deep, watching.

'Namaste,' Ronan ventured. He felt himself redden, but maybe it was just the sun.

They laughed, and then each of them said it. 'Namaste.'

One of them shoved his mate, dunking him under, and soon they were all at it. Diving off each other's shoulders, swimming between legs, flinging each other out to sea. Ronan gave as good as he got. Anywhere else it would have felt gay. They horsed around until the sun began to slip down the sky. One of them held Ronan's arm and turned him towards the sunset.

'West coast, best side,' he explained earnestly.

And he was right. The sky was like nothing Ronan had ever seen before. Ridiculously orange, the water pinky glass. The sun dropped into the sea like a dunked biscuit. Within a minute it was dark. Ronan waded to the water's edge where a silver little fish was flipping out its last seconds of life. He stood watching it. That's what things are like here, he thought, straightforward, dead or alive, black and white, day or night, brilliant, shite. The boys waved him goodbye and headed off in the opposite direction.

'Tomorrow, my friend?' one called out.

'Football?' Ronan shouted after them.

'Yes, football.' Their voices strayed into the night.

With difficulty he found the track back to the hotel. Without light it was a warren; he ended up in several back yards. Families eating, smoky fires, huddles of people chatting at the base of trees. Eyes jumping out of the black of night. He wondered whether goats sleep.

When he got to the road, the place was hopping: cars, rickshaws, motorbikes, bicycles, cows. All whizzing up and down. Barely a light between them. Music and food smells drifted on the breeze. The neck girl wafted out the gateway of the hotel wrapped around what must've been her boyfriend. Chloe popped into Ronan's mind. Oh yeah, Chloe. She did have great breasts but no neck to speak of. Still, he thought, maybe he'd send her a card. The security guard appeared out of nowhere and grabbed Ronan's shoulder, stopping him in his tracks.

'Be careful, Sir. Please. A frog,' he whispered, pointing at the ground.

One more step and Ronan would've stamped on it. Squashed it to death underfoot. Only then did he realise he'd left his runners on the beach.

POEMS IN TRANSLATION
HARIS VLAVIANOS

(from *Sonnets of Despair: apologia pro vita et arte mea*)

8

One way out: draw on the same material
again and again until it sickens.
Has this not happened with Sikelianos?
You read him almost every night for five years
(that damned book published by Galaxy—
didn't it throw all sorts of adolescent plans into the air?),
and now can't stand the sight of his face on the flyleaf.
Every time someone asks the question
you respond awkwardly:
'Yes, yet in volume five, "The Suicide of Atzesivano"…'
as if such predictable evasions can raise his spirit.
Angelos flies off, never to return,
taking with him those grandiose plans.

More to the right, please! He was always *contre lumière*.

9

They waited for it. For you to slip.
And in a silly way you slipped.
Now they spit in the well
you spent twenty years digging in order to draw clean water.
Appropriating? Converting? Not referencing properly
(out of a deep resentment for boorish fellow-travellers)? Does it matter?
'I scarred you for life' is what Hardy wrote in *Jude*.
The final separation scene brought you to tears.
Cry away, because there is no forgiveness for this.
Shakespeare, Celan, Brecht, and so many more,
but these are just excuses. We said it: 'scarred for life'.

Out of the corner of your eye you spy a sparrow
perched on a quivering branch.
Whatever lives lives alone. Time to move on.

Translated from the Greek by Evan Jones

Mill Wheel At Bantry

i.m. J.G. Farrell

This twelve-foot torque is the iron ghost
of an ancient wheel, turning riveted slats
back and up. Now stuck, now moving again
scattering jewels through bright air
from a twist-stream bucketing
over slimed rock by the Library,
combing tangled grass to emerald hair.

This gash at the top of town, with its whiff
of Hades, is where we catch our glimpse
of what's below. From here on down, we join
the hectic flow to the ordinary: tarmac, the Spar
and chip-shops, the cafés and whispering
silver-and-isinglass mud of Bantry Bay.
But churning or still, fortune's wheel

sets the pace. And this wet rock, grey
as a sea lion taking a dive to the dark,
plus this pour-down of spark-froth entering town
by way of the burying ground, run under it all:
under Vickery's and the famine graves,
under the boarded-up House of Elegance,
the fire station and two-room museum

offering memorabilia of martyrs, butter-making,
caring for sheep and photos of where we are
as it used to be; reports of sea-wrecks
and sea-rescue; the resin replica of a cross
descrying the quest of St Brendan
for Isles of the Blest. There's been so much
I haven't attended to. So much I didn't see.

Ruth Padel

Pilgrimage
Suzanne Power

As we come into dock the boat shudders. Jet skiers ride the leading edge of the ferry's wake, cutting inwards to the centre of the back wash. They turn in midair, submerging in the rough edges of wave. I keep count to see how many surface, before going to the foot passenger exit.

My husband Martin and I were that active. Sometimes I let myself remember. Now I can sit for hours. I will look at the clock and it will be evening. Back then I might have preferred to stay at home on weekends too. I was good with my hands. We had a house that required modernisation but ended up getting tradesmen in. Martin's time cost twice as much as theirs. I understood the logic, but never the reasoning. When we had a boundary dispute Martin drove in stakes. The neighbour tore them out. Martin called the land registry. A letter came to say he was right.

'I never argue unless I am.'

We rarely argued. Maybe our children knew this, tolerating outdoor pursuits as something we should enjoy. It did keep us together as a family. It was good for us. But often one or other of them would turn to me and say:

'Tell him to let us go home now. Please.'

Some years ago I sat in front of a woman to seek help by sharing this kind of detail. When I couldn't find words, she asked:

'Are you lost in it? The story?'

*

At Fishguard I find the café just off the road to St David's. John chose it. It doesn't get ferry passengers. I know he would meet me at the dock but I walk to shake off the feelings of the boat. There is a moment when we pull back from Rosslare that I hope never to see it again, then a moment when I step off at Fishguard when I want to be back in Rosslare.

I pass the grander houses of Fishguard built to take Victorians who took the sea air. Martin and I sold our version of these in Wexford town, making a profit from the renovations others did on our behalf. We got out before the economic fall.

On the walk up to the café I think this might be the year I don't want food and don't want to see him. Seeing John has the same effect each time. I feel nauseous in the seconds before I open the café door. As soon as I lay eyes on him I settle into a calm.

'Susan,' he stands up and holds both of my hands with warmth and no pressure. The lady behind the counter has a different apron but the skirt is the same one she had on last year. Her tablecloths are still blue and lemon check. I breathe a sigh of relief that she got rid of the artificial flowers. Those things empty me out.

It's always the same. I think I am never going to eat the scones and tea and jam. I eat the lot. I haven't an appetite at any other time.

I know I'm speaking because I'm hearing John's replies. Whatever I'm saying mostly I am noticing the changes in him in the intervening year. He has gone greyer, his shoulders are still the kind that jackets and sleeves ride up on, leaving his wrists bare. There's a light patch of skin on his left one. He's removed his watch. Last year he kept glancing at it. I thought all of that day this would be our last time.

As I was leaving again he took my hands and his palm skin felt like rocks. His work must be hard. I don't know what he does. I know he stopped driving for a living. What does anyone do? I never think to ask about jobs anymore.

'I'll be here next year,' he told me then.

And he is. And it's the same feeling: his body not fitting his clothes, his lined and kind face, the way he holds quiet until I come through with words. People don't give me long enough. My words aren't close.

'How's Martin, still working hard?' He always asks one question about him.

'Tireless.' Suddenly I can hear myself again. Martin's name still makes me try harder. I know he's doing well, even though I no longer know him.

'You're looking good Susan,' The only lie John ever tells. I see myself in windows sometimes. My eyes are too big for my face. I don't keep mirrors. Other people's fragile inner ghost is hidden; mine has become who I am. I reach into my rucksack.

'They're beautiful.' He takes them from me, considers both. This year's colours are deep skies close to night. I used yellow thread as a contrast, running a shoal of swimming stars and it's this you notice first, but the depth comes from the darkness pushing the light. I spend the hours I can't sleep weaving, then unravelling and weaving again. My mind is soft and sometimes I can't see them anymore. My fingers reach a better understanding of my children. I've used woollens for the first time from their jumpers. I didn't know how to use them before this year; the colours in them were so dark. Then the skies that were in their minds came to me. I've tried to give them those again.

The year I first brought tapestries John put his face in his hands for a long time. But when he looked up his eyes were dry. Later I wrote him a letter. *I had no wish to put you into any further distress. I used to be good with my hands.* He wrote back reassuring me. Later I also got a letter from John's wife. I had no right to put him through this. Did I see what I was doing to her and their children? Did I see?

The following year after receiving their separate letters I changed the date to my children's shared birthday, catching a taxi from the port. John was waiting for me at the holy wellspring.

'How did you know I'd be here today?'

'I've been every day this month. I'd knew they were May children. Did you bring any more of the cloths? I can tie them for you.'

I've let him ever since. He ties them among the other votive rags hanging on the branches, each representing a wish or a longing. Then we drink water so cold it would make you faint, so new to the air it has the taste of soil in it. Water the saints drank to replenish their tired souls and give the tired people who followed them new purpose in its blessing.

I've come on their birthday ever since. He tells his wife he is working and she's chosen to believe him.

*

There is no more tea in the pot. I hug the last drop. The café owner has a habit of ignoring me and talking to John when he pays. They chat in Welsh. It sounds like a song poem to me. All that language. It's comforting that I don't understand and am not required to join in.

'Ready?' He puts my rucksack into the backseat. They're there. Fresh, fragrant and dying. They empty me out. I want to ask him not to bring them, but he is so good.

We drive along the old pilgrim route into St David's, a tiny place made a city by its sacred reputation, past the Cathedral which at this time is chiming for prayer. For thousands of years people have walked this way, carrying sunset shells to indicate hope that once their prayers reached the city shadows would fall behind them. The shells were left in holy wells. This area is full of them, dedicated to many saints. Fragments still surface today of shells cast and cloths tied to branches when a pilgrimage here was worth the same as travelling to Rome. A tapestry of broken people and their long dreams, woven over thousands of years. The well of St Non's, mother of David, is on the city outskirts. When she was pregnant she had a vision and fled to Brittany to raise him, dying there because she could not go home and watch her son fall on hard times. She raised him to his own choices.

We go to her statue and I hold her weeping hands, their plaster bubbling with the effect of winter storms. I take off the snails crawling up her robes and across her face looking for shelter from the salt winds. The water by her feet speaks asking to be drunk. I do so, after John has given my offerings; braided from all that is left, from the clothes that had no time to become memories. There is never a trace of the tapestries I left last year so I like to think Sean and Leah collect their emblems from the branches and carry them to where they are now. People have been tying cloths here for so long. There has to be a reason.

Then I can sit here for hours, without moving. Sometimes I will look at my watch and find it's evening, John still beside me.

'Ready?' He asks only when I move.

After St Non's Well I can only think of being in that place. As we drive, I know it's right to leave the tapestries with her. I weave what they might be in a new life. This road, to Caerfai Bay, is where they lost all they might be in this one. A laneway that cars struggle to pass on. Hedges on high banks obscure the sea view and stoned fields. Still. Even after all that death. I see the tree again.

Martin, Sean, Leah and Susan. We were on holiday. The expectancies. The bickering. The constant noise from the children they were. I want to wince, to flinch, to pack too much for days that were too full as Martin pushed for strong memories that made our lives justifiable. The tears grow cold on my cheeks they are so slow to come. I am free to feel pain. I become the mother I was: rubbing her face with stress, chastising children. I start to see them. We park near the field gate. John opens it. I am looking at the cold sky. John takes his bouquet from the back seat.

There are times when I feel I was never a mother at all. I would not know what to do now. I would have to learn all over again. Behind the hedging John has placed my quartz boulder by a thin wellspring, one not governed by a presiding saint. My heart is grey-veined now, as stone as this is stone.

Martin and I had meant to stand it in the garden we never landscaped. In Wales you can't make roadside memorials. I never thought I would want one. I used to think of them as garish. But Sean and Leah are here more than anywhere. When I returned home after their death, when the house was stone in its silence without them, I sat in the garden with my back against this rock and did my grieving. And after a year of that it had become my heart. And I could only leave my heart in one place.

I wrote to John and asked if he could have it placed if I had it shipped? He made all the arrangements. The farmer who has a second gate to his field, where my car crashed into his hedging, agreed to let us put it there, once it was not marked in any way and not seen from the road.

Now it stands with a hidden meaning in a landscape littered with such things. But those stones are granite. This quartz, it speaks for the children they were and the place they came from. For millennia Wexford quartz has been brought to holy waters by means of worship. I am part of what is known as St David's Stream, the pilgrims who put their pain and hope into the waters. But I have left all of mine here.

As John places the flowers in cellophane among the wildflowers of Pembrokeshire I think again they are as misplaced as he is in his formal clothes. I know I am also alien. Pilgrims don't belong. They leave their prayers and take their story with them. I am lost in mine. I do not exist without this event. For one day a year when John and I mourn together the children he and I killed.

I don't come on their death day. That will always be a month earlier.

John is singing a Welsh hymn. Outside this time I know he is a good man who lives for music. I have no more details and don't want them. I never ask him what the words mean. I just listen. Your life gathers around things that went wrong, things that shouldn't have happened, things with *if* attached to them.

Martin had his work and all its occupation. Sean and Leah had each other in closeness beyond anything I've known. I felt alone in my family. It was as if they all knew they were going to leave me in the end. If I had been less willing to please, or more willing to please. If I had been more myself. If I hadn't given the children the choice of getting out of canoeing on a damp day, on an angry sea. If I hadn't been a creature of compromise even when I fought with my husband, promising to pick him up when the other canoeists were driving back on a shuttle bus.

The days were damp, sleeping in a tent was excruciating. Sean and Leah were laughing when I told their father I was not going on the water because we'd slept in it. I snapped at them I would never go on a family holiday again. They said I said that every year.

'I can still hear it,' John has finished singing, speaking to me with cut eyes of blue. I know he's waiting for me to answer, but I'm seeing it all again. I'm seeing him without grey hair, slighter built, less crags on his large forehead, his eyes less blue and wider. As he was ten years ago.

I'm seeing Sean and Leah, me turning to chastise them out of their bickering. John was coming in the opposite direction. And he met me, not concentrating, head turned. Nowhere for him to go. Nowhere for us to go. The hedging was too high. Sean and Leah screaming. The tree just watching.

I can still picture Martin canoeing on the swollen sea, being right.

John and I are united in the sound of collision. It leaves you deaf to other sounds. It can only be described as the roar you hear in dreams sometimes. I heard my collar bones snap and the roof cave into my head just behind my ear, like someone starting up a chainsaw.

Pilgrimage

Then a silence broken only with a snipping circular cry. Sean's Gameboy insisting on attention. The children making none. They were not yet eleven. That was next month. There was a long time waiting looking at the cold sky before they gouged me out. I feel there were hands pulling me out. I feel they were John's hands. But he was already in an ambulance.

*

On the ferry this morning I met a woman with a small baby, a toddler and a pushchair. I didn't take the boy's hand on the staircase, I took the pushchair instead. I am not capable of certain acts: driving, keeping company, holding the golden hands of other children.

Martin buried ours without me. I got home to find their grave full of fresh cut bouquets that had withered and some gaudy artificial flowers. I stared at their shared birthday and death date on the wooden cross and I couldn't relate to this squared plot holding my children's remains.

'There is no necessity to visit where they died. You're only visiting your own guilt.' Martin only argued when he was right.

So I went alone on their first anniversary.

John was there with his bouquet of flowers. I understand roadside memorials now. This is where the last breath happened. I wish it had taken mine too. Each year I hope my breath will stop, but it continues.

'Ready to go,' I say it to John though I could stay there with him every day until I finally die.

It's a silent journey back to Fishguard. John drops me to the dock and I don't look back or I'd never leave. On the ferry home I watch mothers wince at prices and the noise of their children. I have not seen Martin for eight years. He sent me e-mails and cards at one time. That has stopped.

There was only one occasion I stayed in Wales overnight. John wrote beforehand to tell me about a concert at St David's Cathedral. *Fantasia on a Theme by Thomas Tallis* by Vaughan Williams: *I know it will move you and hearing it has been of benefit to me.*

I am not capable of certain acts and don't enjoy the disappointments I create. But he never put any other request. I thought I could help him by pretending it helped me.

The *Fantasia* caught all the whispers of all despair, heard and held by the medieval stone. It caught mine. I saw the children watching me, in the time where they came to an end and I came to an end. I wanted to turn to John and ask him why have you brought me to this? But I saw Martin's face in the music suddenly. I saw his struggle not to hate me. When I woke in the hospital he was by my bedside, having already been to the morgue.

'The driver of the van says it's his fault.'

I told him what he most hates to hear. So he took my children home and buried them without me. While I recovered in the Welsh hospital I had one visitor, who kept me company each day, for one hour. We spoke of nothing. We sat together. It was the first of the remembering.

Then in one great note the music took us out of the pain to the dreaming. I saw the chaos of the world made serene by the distance a sky provides. I watched my children, lifted off the suffering road into the skies in their minds.

I thirst for a chance to catch sight of them as adult beings, progressing into futures, taking on burdens. I walk with their loss as mine. It is a loss I cannot put down. I listened to the music holding their lost souls and felt mine held too.

John turned in the long silent moment after the music and gave me the mourning in his eyes. It has made them bluer. He takes me to the well each year because he doesn't want me to get lost in the story. He says he will always visit Sean and Leah, but he hopes one day I won't have to, that their memory will be enough. That my life will bring more.

These are its remains. I live each year for one day. I ask myself if John disappeared would I make the same pilgrimage? It means more with his presence. We shared the darkest moment and we continue to share it. For one day I am not silent.

On all others I want to tell every mother I meet I was one too.

Insomniac Mothersong

All the disasters you anticipate
rear up at once, each time you close your eyes.
There's nothing you can do, just lie awake.

Your guts churn, but it's not something you ate,
it's just the strain of cutting down to size
all the disasters you anticipate.

Don't fuss, don't worry, don't exaggerate—
you soothe yourself with reassuring lies.
It doesn't help. You know you'll stay awake.

They're only young, they'll learn from their mistakes
—but it's their childish hubris that gives rise
to these disasters you anticipate.

They rush at things, they don't know how to wait.
Don't question them, they'll only tell you lies.
They don't know it's their fault you stay awake.

And if their lives heave like a small earthquake,
how can you mitigate or minimise
all the disasters you anticipate?
There's nothing you can do. Just stay awake.

Janet Shepperson

Lighting Fires on the Moon

'Firefighters have battled more than 700 gorse fires here in just 10 days'
—*Belfast Telegraph,* 28th April 2011

It starts with a rustling in the gorse, a hint
of orange-yellow you could warm your hands by.
It escalates into *colossal flames,*
moving faster than a man could run
on a flat road, let alone up in the hills.
When you dropped the lighter and empty petrol can
and got the hell out, what did you have in mind—
adrenaline rush, a scene from a horror movie,
a wild and glorious trail of beacon fires
screaming that the Germans are coming, the Russians,
the Orcs from *Lord of the Rings*? What you imagined
couldn't have been this grey contorted twitching
sprawl of limbs screwed up like dying spiders—
a charred mess. Even the air itself seems scorched,
starved of oxygen. *Moonscape,* say the papers,
something a spacecraft would land on. Then again,
perhaps this was what you wanted all along—
smoke rising from an alien, ashy landscape,
sending a message back to planet Earth
that you were here, spitting defiance, lost
in a wild and endless orbit of loneliness.

Janet Shepperson

Homily (or The Odd Couple)

For Jerzy Popieluszko & Pier Paolo Pasolini

Benedictus qui venit in nominee Domine

I

A breath splits the air at the reservoir like a gunshot.
Laughter floats across the foamy surf like cigarette smoke.
Mute faces, pressed against glass, pass by in an old Polski
Fiat, a Polonez, or Audi. On soundless televisions, moustachioed
men of impossible ethnic extraction—sifted from the Nemen
River, dug from the mud at Katyń, or rounded up in the mountains
of Friuli—smoke disinterestedly. Images flicker. They drag the reservoir.
Young lovers stumble across sodden bundles, tied with twine
like parcels of old clothes, or blood-smeared, sand-caked forms;
mulched eyes and pulped tongues, gruesome death masks.
Once the death rituals have been observed, the purgatorial
are moved, wrapped in plastic; newly-made martyrs,
raised overhead like a chasuble. In death, photography,
though an art and easily replicable, is not simply a diagnostic,
or forensic tool. It fixes you both in time in similar ways,
though you held differing moralities and might not have mourned
each other's passing. Each photograph taken is a step, or a word;
a poem, or a sermon; a film, or a Mass. Magnets for hatred, what
is not understood, certainly by you, Jerzy and Paolo, is that being
tainted by Original Sin is not the worst thing imaginable. There is no
sin in knowledge, or wisdom—in being a heretic, one who seeks
knowledge. The sin is often in truth, though the truth is: a man
will give up his life happily, once he knows what he is dying for.

II

Consider the word *mass*, from your differing perspectives: mass
consumption; mass media; mass market; Mass as mystery; Mass as
consumption of the body; the body and blood transformed into edible
mass. The body subjugated through dogma, religious and political;
the spirit subjugated through ritual. The arm raised, extended, then
beaten against the chest, draws automatically to the sign of the cross.
Listen to me now, you shades in the corner: walk with the wind.
Your hearts no longer beat, are no longer fuelled by human passions;
the heart's windows are no longer battered by storms; you no longer
feel the pain and passion of struggle, the very human struggle for
dignity, you two saints. It is said you looked for death; courted it
as one does a prospective lover; danced with it as one does a virginal
wife on her wedding day. And the parallels? Protest; the fight for the
freedom to enslave yourselves; the closed coffins; the beating of chests;
the crowing from the balconies of Europe, that justice was done. But tell
me this, if you will? Where is the justice in mother's outliving their sons?
On your graves, wild thyme flowers. The past is the past is the past.

J. Roycroft

Mass

Mass will be said for no more bad language and gambling and wanking that the Athenry boys are doing, down the back of the castle, down the back of the couch, all the punching and hitting and groaning, moaning at the Turlough boys, the Clarinbridge boys, the boys from Killimordaly, down the back of the Presentation grounds.

There will be mass when you lose at the Galway Races
and for the saving of your soul if you take the boat to Cheltenham.

There will be a mass for when the horse runs, and when the horse dies,
and for the bookies who win and the punters who win,
and the bookies who lose and the punters who lose.

There will be mass for hare coursing and flask-filling.

There will be mass for your Inter Cert and your twenty-first,
There will be a filling-out-your-CAO-form mass.

Mass will be held in the morning before the exams,
mass will be held in the evening for your bath.

There'll be a special mass on Saturday afternoon for your Granny. There will be a mass for your Granny's boils and aches and black lungs and ulcers and spots and diabetes and psychosis.

There'll be a mass for the anointing of the bollix of the bull above in the field
near the closh over the railway bridge.

Mass will be held before the College's Junior B Hurling Final, it will be held
for the Connaught Cup Junior A Regional Final in wizardry and sarcasm.

Mass will be held on top of the reek for the arrogant and meek, and the bishop will arrive by eurocopter. There will be a mass to get him up in one piece and back in one piece.

Mass will be held in outhouses where children were hung.

Mass will be held for the safe arrival of new lambs and the birthing of ass foals.

Mass will be held in your uncle's sitting room but his neighbours will be envious
and later stage a finer mass.

There will be a mass to find you a husband, and a mass to pray he stays.

There will be a good intentions mass. Your intentions if they're good will come true.

Mass will be held for your weddings and wakes and when you wake up.

Mass will be held for the Muslim's conversion.
Mass will be held for George Bush.
Mass will be held for the war on terror.
Mass will be held for black babies and yellow babies and the yellowy black babies.

Mass will not be held for red babies.
They have upset Pope John Paul.

Mass will be held for your brother when he gets the meningitis from picking his nose.

Mass will be held for your cousins when they stop going to mass.

Mass will be held for a harvest and a sun and a moon and a frost and a snow
and for a healthy spring and red autumn, for a good wind and no wind, and for a
good shower and a dry spell, and for the silage and the hay and the grass and the turf.

There will be a saving-of-the-turf day.
There will be a saving-of-the-hay day.
There will be a saving-my-soul day.

There will a mass for the fishing fishermen.

There will be multiple masses for Mary around August when she did all the appearing.

There will be a good mass when the statue cries rusty tears.
There will be a good mass and a good collection.

Mass will be held for the cloud people, I mean the dead.
Mass will be held for apparitions and anniversaries and weddings and baptisms.

Mass will be held.

There will be mighty masses.

continues...

Mass will be held to church your sinned body after giving birth, there will be mass to wash your unclean feet.

Mass will be held for all your decisions so you don't have to blame yourself.

There will be mass for the dead Poor Clares.
There will be mass for the Black Protestants if Paisley allows it.
Mass will be held for the De Valeras and the Croke Park goers.

There will be a mass for the conversion of the Jews (and their collection).

There will be a mass for the communion class, there will be a mass for the no-name club non-drinkers. There will be a giving-up-smoking-the-Christian-way mass.

There will be a mass for the Christian Angels, only the Christian ones.

There will be no mass for your freedom, no mass, but the air will be sweet as peas and the sky will look clear.

Mass will not be held for the souls of your gay sons.

Mass will not be held for abuse victims, for cynics, anti-clerics, the song-and-dance makers, the antagonising atheists, the upsetting-the-apple-cart persons.

There will be no women's mass.

There will be no mass solely by women for women.

Your daughters will not hold mass.

There are strict rules for mass.

Elaine Feeney

Main Street, Underworld
S.J. Ryan

I hobble down the street of memory. I trip, the paving stones greasy and uneven, flotsam piled in drifts against the pebble dash exterior of the terraced buildings, interrupted by side alleys. I hesitate, catching sight of my reflection in a grubby shop front, chipped mannequins leering from within—here, an adult male grimacing in a child's school uniform and wiry, matted wig—there, the breasts of a bald adult female protruding through a dress shirt, hands folded beneath a striped tie.

A man emerges into the grey overcast day, pushing through double wooden doors that swing and whine, snapping at the tattered tails of his stained coat. I enter. The proprietor is lying on the wooden bar counter wearing a dark suit of clothes, an ironed white shirt and worn, polished shoes. His hands hold a miniature bottle of vodka upright on the barrel of his chest. Beads of sweat glisten on the patina of his skull between strands of black hair that have been combed from one ear to the other.

Steam rises from two aluminium pots on a double hot plate. Beads of water run down the peeling wallpaper. A woman with braided strawberry blonde hair lifts one of the lids and tests the contents of the pot with a knife. She replaces the lid and picks up a viola, cradling it in the crook of her neck above her full white bosom. She tilts her head sideways and looks at me with green eyes, smiling, sweeping the bow across the strings with her right hand, on the ring finger of which there is a golden love knot.

'A pint, please.' My voice rasps like the cry of a rook.

The proprietor clears his throat.

'I have a lip on me like a motherless foal,' he says, taking a sip of vodka, then cocking his head towards the row of pint handles.

'No bother,' says the woman, turning to face the mirrored back of the bar above a glass fronted fridge which displays a carton of milk, a loaf of sliced bread in crumpled greaseproof paper, a block of butter in foil and a jar of jam. Her body is a sickle moon around the sweetly singing viola. Head still slanting sideways she glances left and right at the reflection of people assembled around the u-shaped bar then puts down her instrument and holds a glass at an angle beneath a brass tap, pulling down a white handle which releases a stream of dark liquid that froths as it hits the side. Once the glass is three-quarters full, she puts it to one side and begins to fill another. I watch the creamy head on the gleaming liquid settle.

'Guinness time.' She gives me her sideways smile and tops up the first glass with an angled stream until the head of the pint is thick and creamy. 'Would you like a taste?' she asks, tossing her head towards the hotplate.

'Just a bit.'

She lifts one of the pots with a tea towel and tilts the lid, moving her face out of the path of steam that rises from the boiling water which she drains into a copper sink beneath the bar counter. She puts the pot back on the stove, sticks in a fork and lifts out a floury white potato bursting out of thick brown skin speckled with black spots.

'New Seasons,' she whispers, replacing the lid. She puts the potato on a side plate and drops a knob of butter onto it, then spoons out half a ladleful of food from the second pot. She places the side plate in front of me with a spoon and a fork. I eat. The juice from the ham joint and dark green cabbage is fragrant and salty, the rosy flesh tender and succulent.

The proprietor twitches his moustache.

'A cobbler's children go barefoot,' he says. Without opening his eyes he raises his head and lifts the pint glass which has been placed in his hands to his full lips, raising his little finger as he drains its contents in five swallows. In front of the full-length window, a young man with a worn face squats with an open plastic bag on his knees, scooping out white powder which he inhales directly from his hand. He offers his cupped palm to his female companion, who shakes her head, staring at the floor.

Creatures beat dark wings in my mind. A second drink and I will succumb to their talons, become oblivious to everything but the dizzying heights of their flight until they release me mid-air in order to split open my skull, and I am dashed to the ground with a sour tongue of remorse.

I place my empty glass and some money on the counter and wipe my mouth with the back of my hand.

'None so pure as a converted hoor,' says the proprietor, passing wind.

I walk across the smoky, ill-lit room with its bare concrete floor and metal roof supports and push my way through tacky painted hardboard flaps on rusted hinges. I blink in the glare of daylight. A man with a swollen red face, yellowed whiskers and straggling white hair is waving a plastic mug at vehicles moving down the street. He shouts unintelligibly, a bottle of cider on the pavement behind him. He lurches towards me. An odour of bile and urine rises from him and I pull my coat lapels together, stepping to one side in order to pass.

'Where're ye off to?' he cries.

Though uncertain of my destination, I quicken my pace. I roll and tumble with the slipstream of the street. At first the flow of traffic propels me forward. Debris knocks against, then covers, me—a rusted car door, the chassis of a truck, a bent fender, a cracked rear-view mirror, a shattered windscreen limp inside its rubber casing. I attempt to surface but am struck by wooden planks, cast-off rubber retreads, metal pram wheels, bicycle tyres and jagged umbrella spokes. The warped hand-tooled wheel of a cart hooks me, broken crockery scrapes me, remnants of garments and shoes graze me—a leather boot with no laces, bent upwards at the toe, a child's raspberry and white striped woollen mitten, a red plastic purse, a silver hairclip. Torn and empty plastic animal feed and coal sacks, polystyrene containers, faded newspaper and wrinkled greaseproof covers from long-since digested meals wrap around me but the pressure from behind is too strong, the peristalsis churns and presses until I shoot forward from the blockage hindering my progress.

I find myself at the feet of a middle-aged man. He turns around and looks down at me, nods, then stares ahead, a folded newspaper under his arm. I stand up and lean out from behind his anorak-clad back and realise that I am at the rear of a queue of people which extends around a corner. We shuffle forward. People driving past crane their necks, staring at us. Some in the queue hunch their shoulders, pull their chins into their chests and look down at the pavement. Others wear sunglasses though the sun is not shining, or pull umbrellas low across their faces.

We pass a bookmaker's shop. People cut through the queue in order to enter, the door banging behind them. They throw crumpled pieces of paper on the ground as they leave. Next is the location of an antique dealer. I attempt to avert my eyes but am drawn by the interior scene. A man at the rear of the shop opens a glass case. A woman in a fur coat and leather gloves stands next to him. The man holds up stainless steel instruments of amputation to the electric light, then hands them to the woman, who examines them closely. She selects three, which he wraps in brown paper. Reflected in the window from a corner opposite, two small dogs mate on the pavement.

After an hour, my position has advanced and I approach the doorway on the street into which the queue disappears. People have continued to line up behind me since I first took my place. I look back and cannot see where it ends.

Glad to be out of the view of passers-by I enter a small room which contains a wooden counter with three partitions. The letters 'A – M' are written on a sheet of paper taped below the furthest counter, the letters 'N – Z' below the middle one. A woman stands behind the third counter paging through forms and avoiding eye contact. There is no one behind the first or the second counter, the latter being the one I assume I should approach, as the letters on the sign include that with which my surname begins. I wait for what I consider to be a respectable period of time and then look at the woman.

'Excuse me,' I say. The woman ignores me.

Two teenage girls in velour tracksuits and fabric ankle boots burst into the room, each pushing a pram. Wearing hoop earrings and rings on most of their fingers, they smell of fried food and are conversing loudly. The woman behind the counter looks

Main Street, Underworld

up and smiles, extending a hand to indicate that they should approach. Their toddlers bawl and arch their backs. The girls sign papers handed to them by the woman. She asks them for certain documentation which they say they do not have but are told not to worry and to come straight back to the counter when they return with it. The queue moves to one side to allow them to leave. The man behind me shifts his weight from one foot to the other.

Encouraged by the woman's changed manner I approach her.

'I'm not open,' she says.

'Which counter should I go to?' I ask.

'You'll have to wait. They're in the back.'

The man behind me pushes forward.

'I've had enough!' he shouts. 'I haven't worked for two months.' He punctuates the air in front of the woman's face with a pointed finger. 'I've been coming down to this office every week and waiting for hours in the street. Each time I come down I'm given a different story. I've got bills to pay, children to feed, a car to fix. I've been paying my unemployment insurance for twenty-two years and I'm sick of this!' A vein is raised on the side of his forehead.

The woman's face is expressionless.

'Where's your card?' she asks the man. He hands her a plastic card and she flicks through a cardboard box containing alphabetically-ordered index cards.

'You're not in here,' she says. The man's breathing is laboured. His neck is red.

'Oh, I see they've put you in the wrong place,' she says, pulling out a card, 'sign here.' She pushes a pen towards the man, pointing at a space on the index card with an acrylic fingernail.

The man signs the card and is told to return the following week. He leaves, his shoulders slumped, and I follow him out.

We are struck by an avalanche of paper as we step into the street. Bank statements, accounts, printed forms, tax returns, receipts, curriculum vitae, insurance claim forms, job applications and debit order authorisations engulf us. Letters of demand, invoices, school reports, certificates, draft separation agreements, income and expense statements, rejection letters, sick notes and prescriptions weigh us down. I crawl on my belly to get away from the man, whose load of paper is even heavier than mine.

I look up and see that I am directly in front of the stuccoed façade of a bank. I stand, brush myself off and enter through its carved stone pillars.

The interior is air-conditioned. My movements are monitored by a security camera that whirrs and clicks in a corner, near the ceiling. A man unclips the brass hook of a rope partition suspended between waist-high poles, bowing as I pass through. I notice a splash of blood on the polished marble floor.

I inhale sharply as I feel a stinging sensation in my upper arm. Turning my head I see the man withdrawing the needle of a hypodermic syringe from where he has jabbed it through my sleeve. His face appears to twist and distort as I fall to the ground, paralysed but conscious. People in white coats and surgical masks appear from a door in a wood-panelled wall. They lift me onto a trolley and wheel me down a corridor, their rubber-soled shoes silent.

We pass a doorway with a sign which reads 'Personal Loans'. Inside I see a woman in a dental chair, a row of bloody canine teeth on a metal tray next to her. Further on is a doorway displaying the name 'Remortgaging'. It contains rows of people lying on folding beds, needles in their arms attached to plastic tubes leading to blood bags suspended above their heads.

The trolley turns a corner. As I am wheeled through a doorway I notice a sign above it that says 'Arrears'. I am placed under a bright light and my clothes are removed. People peer down at me in masks and gowns, signalling to each other with their eyes. I see the glint of a scalpel and am aware of a pressure against the skin below my ribcage. My torso moves up and down as gloved hands push and search inside the cavity of my chest.

Something is removed from my body and dropped into a white enamel kidney dish. I catch sight of the glistening organ as it is weighed, then placed in the drawer of a filing cabinet. In exchange I am given a bank card, which is slipped inside a plastic wallet and placed on my pillow. I am wheeled into a corner of the room as another trolley is wheeled in.

When I regain my senses I am in a small wooden boat, dressed once more. My tongue feels thick in my dry mouth. My head and body ache. A hooded figure stands in the prow, rowing with a long oar. We float down the rising current of the main street.

We sail past a butcher's shop with salted pork and black and white puddings hanging in the window from metal hooks. We pass a church networked with scaffolding. In the churchyard two boys clean gravestones then lean against the church wall, tie tourniquets around their upper arms and inject needles into their soft white skin. We drift past a housing estate and glimpse young men in nylon tracksuits and shaved heads brandishing swords in a concreted clearing.

The boat reaches the opposite side of the street and I disembark.

Weak with pain, I limp towards the only person in sight. His body is lean, with a slackness of skin around the neck. Present with his work at hand, he power-hoses the pavement outside a semi-detached house. He is cross-eyed and when I speak to him I attempt to look into one eye, but find my focus moving between the two.

'Where should I go?' I ask.

'You must decide,' he says, looking in two different directions at once.

I force my limbs to move until I reach a side street. I see mountains in the distance, trees reaching into the sky against the horizon. The sun breaks through scattered clouds. I take a step on the route leading to the valley which lies ahead, staggering at first, then gaining momentum as my heartbeat quickens. I recognise the path, realise I am retracing my steps. Striding briskly, I weep. I make my way towards the home I had left, to discover what remains.

Main Street, Underworld

An Casán Dearg

Tuigim
Anois,
Is dóigh liom,
Ná fuil maith
Dom
Sa chásán
A dheargaíos
Go doras
Do thí
Gan tú
Ar a cheann
Ná
Ar a bhun.
Ní fheadar
Anois
Cad a thug mé
Fiú
Ar teachtaireacht
Nach cuimhin liom,
Im strainséar
Ar eachtra
I dtír aineoil an chroí.

Tesco

Portráidí an chumha
Aithním gan dua
Dúmas gur bua,
Mo mhéar fós fliuch ón umar,
Bas le héadan,
Clais sa ghrua,
Roc sa mhala,
An tsúil a scréachann,
An uillinn ghéar,
An ghnúis a doirteadh fé aidhl a dó.

Fé cheilt an chealtair
Ní lámh dá chéile
Ná céile do láimh,
Ní ligimíd ar a chéile sin
Ní bheannaímíd,
Súil suas, siúil síos,
Súil síos, siúil suas,
Caochóga ar an gcóisir
Ó arán go hubh
In Tesco inniu.

Stiofán Ó Cadhla

The Red Path

I know now,
I think,
How wayward
My way,
Worn red
To the door
Of your house
When you are
No longer
At either end.
Now I even wonder
Why I came,
For what unremembered
Message,
A stranger
In the uncharted land
Of the heart.

Tesco

Sorrow's portraits
I now know
By mere shape alone
As a gift,
My finger still wet from the font,
Hand to head
Creased cheek
Chink in brow,
The eye that screams,
Pent elbow
And visage spilled in the aisle.

Masqued
Neither hand to hold
Nor chaperone
Neither meeting,
Nor greeting,
Eyes up, walking down,
Eyes down, walking up,
Unsighted, unseen,
Between the eggs and bread
Astray
In Tesco's today.

Translated from the Irish by Stiofán Ó Cadhla

Fuascailt Nell Crane

Nell Crane, m'ainmse,
an t-aon rud nár athraigh
ó bhuail mé liom féin i súil tairbh.
Bhí mo dhroim le falla agam
mar rialaíonn an cruinne seo falla amháin do lucht na teipe.
Sea, mo dhroim le falla is mé ag cuimhneamh
ar na fir nár spéis leo riamh mé—
is na mná sásta go raibh an iomaíocht laghdaithe,
mar aon leis an stair a ghabh tharam ar chapall,
an chinniúint ar traein,
an t-ádh i Maserati
agus an future nar tháinig riamh.
Sea, mo dhroim le falla
ach domsa stad an saol de bheith am chrá
an lá a ghabhas an cóngar tré ghort Shanahan
is gan mé ach tríocha is a trí
agus gach bliain díobh díolta go maith as
ach nuair a thosaigh an talamh ar crith im dhiaidh,
thuigeas go raibh compánach agam
is ansan an bhúir, íseal, leathan, ón saol eile
sin an uair a thuig mé nár bhaol dom.
Agus ansan a anáil the ar m'ioscaidí arís is arís
Is níor ritheas mar cé rithfeadh ó leannán?

Ó rugadh mé níor dhein éinne mé a chosaint go dtí anois
Ach anois bhí fáinne práis im shrón agam
Is mé ag séideadh anála fén saol.
Sea, bhíos tréis casadh orm féin don gcéad uair
agus b'fhiú an aithne.
Shéid sé anáil arís, níos teo
agus an bhúir ní ba dhoimhne.
Rithfeadh an focal grámhar leat
agus b'shin mar a bhí, an bheirt againn ag tógaint an chóngair—
mise i gcoiscéimeanna, eisean ag tuargaint an talaimh
is mo bharraicíní ag síneadh is ag crapadh.

Nuair a léimeas thar díog Shanahan,
d'fhéach mé air don gcéad uair agus bhí cuma chrosta air
ach crostacht don saol ab ea é agus é tuillte acu.
Bhí iarracht de lán orm
mar b'é seo tús le laochas.
D'fhéachas níos doimhne ina shúile órga
agus láithreach thuig mé go bhfuil an saol ar fad ceapaithe
agus gach rud socair ann—fiú amháin Nell Crane—
Bhí sé chomh soiléir le clog glé an tsléibhe
a rá liom gur liom an saol chomh maith le cách.

Na laethe seo nuair a bhím in aice móinéir
cuimhním ar mo thairbhín is é go glúin i mbláthá samhraidh
agus solas ón saol eile ag briseadh tréna shúilibh
agus tuigim gur i súil tairbh
a cheileann an Nádúr
ár ndaonnacht.

Seán MacMathúna

The Release of Nell Crane

My name is Nell Crane, the only thing that hasn't changed
since I first met myself
in the eye of a bull.
I had a wall to lean on
for this universe ordains that all failures are given a wall.
so, I leaned and the more I leaned,
the more wall-like I became
and transparent so they can look through you
and the women glad of one less in the field—
as was history that passed by on a horse,
destiny in a train,
fate in a Maserati,
and the future never came.
So, I leaned.
But for me the wall vanished
the day I took the shortcut
across Shanahan's field
and me just thirty-three
and each year dearly paid for.
But when the ground behind me
began to shake,
I knew I had a guest.
And when the bellow lowed
as if from another world,
that's when I knew there was no need for fear,
then the hot breath
all over the backs of my knees, again and again.
The first time no one saw me, the second time I didn't care,
I did not run—
who runs from a lover?

I had never before felt protected: now I had a brass ring in my nose
And I snorted steam at the world.
I became me for the first time.
He blew breath again and it was great
after thirty years of the wall.
And the bellows became more intimate
and each bellow meant for me
and there we were crossing the field together,
I mincing, he shaking the earth
and my toes open and shut.

I leaped across Shanahan's dyke
and I turned for the first time. He looked cross but that was a crossness
for a world that deserved it.
I looked deep into his golden eyes
and suddenly I knew that all that is
was meant to be,
including Nell Crane.
It had the clarity of a mountain bell
that rang all the way across my awakening world
showing me what was mine at last.

These days when I pass a meadow,
I picture him standing knee-deep in summer flowers,
his eyes calm and commanding
for it is in the eye of a bull
that Nature hides our humanity.

Translated from the Irish by Seán MacMathúna

Morning, 1908
Claire-Louise Bennett

Since he'd advised it, and it had immediately appeared perfectly rational—to the point of being really rather obvious—I filled a glass with tap water and took a few sips. I imagine his idea was that I drink a full glass, but I just wasn't able to stomach it all, not then. Nevertheless, the little amount I did manage was really very refreshing—uplifting actually—and the dizziness that had bristled in and about my joints since I'd got up out of bed more or less subsided directly after consuming it. That done, and better oriented, I took a long thin coat from the wardrobe, toppling a patent leather Tricker's boot from the shelf to the floor as I did so, and put it on over my dressing gown and night slip. No one will see me, I thought, but took a look in the mirror near the door all the same. And was surprised to see that the three garments layered this way looked very well, rather pretty actually, and I evaluated, briefly, if I couldn't perhaps wear the ensemble publicly—on a Saturday, for example, when I go about my business, such as it is, in the town—before swiftly conceding that France, in fact, was just about the only place where I might feel comfortable in such an outfit, and on any given day.

This is my favourite time to leave the house and take a slow short walk. It is the time when my mind is least disposed towards fuss or hypothesis. It is the time when I have nothing to do after. Even so, I wasn't expecting much from it this evening—I don't know why. Possibly because I was taking one thing at a time and therefore such a thing as expectation was nigh on impossible to cultivate. Added to which, the impetus, really, for being out there at all was primarily to take some new air, and, secondly, to have my body undergo a little activity, however gently, however briefly. Pragmatic objectives, then, pertaining to my physical well-being, were my principal concern—I was not, for example, looking to overhaul my mental disposition or redirect my emotional bearings. To be perfectly honest I have, of late, become unusually disassociated from my immediate surroundings. The weather has not been co-operative this summer and such is my resignation that recently I have taken to commenting upon it in routine phrases which demonstrate exasperation and contempt while leaving the utter indifference I've actually begun to feel towards it undetected and intact. It just never stops. Standing next to where the trees are particularly dense, long after the downpour has expired, you could be forgiven for thinking it was still raining. But in fact what you'd be hearing is just the sound of raindrops sliding off one leaf down to the next, and so on, from leaf to leaf to leaf, until falling, finally, from the last leaf to the ground.

Incredible, really. Or so it seemed to me as I went by and heard the thing play out. Further along there were those very small raindrops, droplets I suppose, which attach themselves with resolute but nonetheless ebullient regularity among the fronds of a beautiful type of delicate grass, appearing, for all the world, like a squandered chandelier dashing headlong down the hillside. I soon came to stand by one of the gates for a while, one I ordinarily pass by in fact—most times there's a wind blowing up here, and, regardless of its provenance, it invariably travels through the gate in such a way as to take a sound from it. The same sound always. A sound I don't mind hearing incidentally, while moving, but which would, I'm sure, induce a kind of peripheral insanity if attended to in stationary fashion for very long. Still, despite the gate being uncommonly mute, I would not describe the time I allotted to spend there as being altogether peaceful. The first thing to occur was not the first thing to happen—however, the manner by which it came to be, and the aberrant mode of analysis it incited, gave it a primacy that is almost as indecipherable as it is indelible.

I'm used to vehicles coming up this way. That is something I am used to. And sometimes—though less often—they go down the way, and I'm used to that too. In either case I step into the long grass, out of the way. At such times he, without fail, would put a hand up to the driver, whereas I never would—I don't know why and I do know why. I'm just the same, actually, when I'm on my own, but maybe the reason is different then. Or maybe it wouldn't seem correct to do a thing without him that I do not do with him.

I don't know and don't believe scrutinising these minor characteristics is a worthwhile pursuit just now—the point is, no car came by. Not one, not in either direction. A car passing by me is something I am accustomed to—a young man passing by me on this road, on the other hand, is something I am not at all accustomed to. So it was that while I stood at the gate there came up the road not the thing I am accustomed to but its opposite, a young man, on foot, his head in a hood. An apparition quite without precedence. I saw him and I almost didn't believe it. I saw him, the young man, and it was an alarming thing. A most alarming thing. And yet it didn't feel as if the alarm I was experiencing had originated from me—it was rather as if I was implementing the feeling for some sort of external design. No, it didn't quite belong to me, and in fact it didn't quite belong to the situation either—as the young man came closer the sensation did not increase, as one would expect, but stayed the same—as such I could only infer that the alarm I was undergoing was probably not attributable to the young man's presence entirely.

It seemed to me very likely that on a different day a sighting of this sort would have exerted nothing greater than a slight and wholly mundane influence upon my awareness. Howsoever, as it was, this was not a different day, but precisely the same day I'd been having since I'd left the house. And everything between leaving the house and coming to stop at the gate had transmitted such a subdued yet supernaturally ominous intensity that one could very well be inclined to intuit that some sort of shattering catastrophe, one that had been amassing for a very long time, was now on the brink of executing an atrocious palpability.

I angled my elbows upon the gate's top railing so that my hands tilted back behind my ears and my fingers slid up into my hair, and I committed every bone to this position despite not being entirely satisfied with it. Initially I thought it might signal an impenetrable insularity—to the point of rendering me invisible perhaps—but this rather abstract musing was emphatically quashed by the terrible realisation that actually I in fact appeared as defenceless and available for the taking as an ostracised vole. Unable to withstand or accommodate the alarm that was becoming more and more exacting, I found myself attempting to counter it with the idea that perhaps the worst thing that could happen might not be quite as diabolical and frenzied as the thought of it jaggedly decreed. If it— that—were to happen, would it be so awful, I thought. Would it really be such an upheaval—such a defiling affront? Perhaps on the contrary, I thought, it might actually seem fairly recreational, like the way dogs are, and not the least bit vile. And then after a moment of blank thought it occurred to me that I'd very likely wet myself. That was a certainty, more or less, and it troubled me actually. The likelihood that I'd wet myself—not after the assault, but during—troubled me. I figured it would be unavoidable really, because, for one thing, of all the rainwater that entwined in a lithe stream along the side of the road, and, for another thing—though I drank very little water before leaving the house earlier, I had in fact consumed a considerable quantity of ginger tea throughout the afternoon—consequently my bladder was already very susceptible.

What do you care, I thought, if you urinate on him during? Wouldn't it serve him right? I did not dwell upon the question long because the fact of the matter was that the idea of urinating on him bothered me very much, and I did not, just then, wish to confront the reason why. As his proximity to me increased I became aware of myself from the young man's perspective—my shabby sealskin boots, the cerise snowflake pattern around the top of my thick Norwegian socks, the thin lace trim along the hem of my nightdress. My damp unbrushed hair. Nothing happened of course. I stood at the gate and a young man passed by. That was all.

Then the cows went all queer on me. That was the second thing to happen. When I first arrived at the gate, which was in fact a good while before I'd seen the young

Claire-Louise Bennett

man, the cows had sort of scarpered off to the left side of the field, down a kind of gradient—a reaction which, in itself, wasn't very remarkable so I accorded it no significance and mention it now only in order to clarify the herd's temperament and position so that the subsequent development, convoluted as it was, may be better appreciated. I didn't mind in the least that the cows took exception to my approach, and found myself likening them to a shoal of fish on account of the way they each stared out at me from just one side of their head as they ran by. In fact, if anything, I rather approved of their taking up a more distant location since it meant my attention was free to overlook them. However, this modest reprieve did not last long—soon after the young man had passed by me, and my hands sunk down from behind my ears—the cows drew in close to one another and all looked up at me with the very same expression. I wondered what exactly they could see, and did not move. Some time passed, right up against me, and then the cows moved forward a little more—all of them still regarding me with that same expression.

They stopped and continued several times over and always in the same rhythm, and even though, as they got nearer, I became a little uneasy, I managed, actually, to maintain my position at the gate. In all this time they did not take their eyes away from me, and so unwavering was this confluence of looking that I went on wondering what exactly it was they could see. Once they got fairly close they became less unified— some were genuinely nervous, while others merely followed suit, and at least one was acquiring that lurching confidence which menial and unexamined curiosity brings out in certain members of any species. I must admit that all this had me feeling fundamentally discomposed in a way I could not describe or even classify. However, despite my inadequate comprehension of the situation and its consequences it was somehow clear to me that something was going on and so I continued to stand where I was and remained there until the one cow reached across the gate with his nostrils and released a long sultry breath across the backs of both my hands—at which point I couldn't see that there was anything left to do. The situation, whatever it was, seemed at an end—although the outcome, whatever that was, had perhaps yet to begin— and so I stepped back from the gate, not quite ceremoniously, but with what I felt to be due consideration. Once I found myself to be very much back within the parallel parameters of the narrow road I turned then and slowly carried on up the hill.

It must have been the case that after the strangely contracted interaction with the cows I needed a much vaster, more general, and completely disinterested picture to reassert itself because I began to extend a scoping look about me. A survey that might well have encompassed the broad and familiar panorama that is available from this vantage point had it not stalled upon the figure of the young man, who now stood facing northwest beneath the mast on top of the hill.

There wasn't much opportunity this time for me to get worked up about his appearance, because almost immediately I saw him a line of smoke distended from

Morning, 1908

his mouth and gave me to suspect he'd recently had some perennial and debilitating misunderstanding with someone close to him—a girlfriend, or his father—I couldn't quite make up my mind which. This notion of mine did much to humanise the young man, of course, and so I continued up the hill without my recently rehearnessed equability becoming compromised or any unchartered area of my psyche enforcing abrupt and unmitigated sway. As I rounded the bend the atmosphere was very much involved in a customary process of change, and in fact some way past the Maamturks there was a sunset beginning. Beginning very modestly, it ought to be said, and then, via a series of protracted and imperceptible increments, acquired the trenchant beauty and dubious brilliance of a new and unnamed world. And so it was I came to linger within the vicinity of another gate. I did not approach this one. There was no need. No need, now, to angle my elbows upon a gate and have my hands recline and disappear.

Everyone has seen a sunset. I will not attempt to describe how this one went. Neither will I set down any of the things that surged to mind when the earth's trajectory became so discernibly and disarmingly attested to. Alien things, yet intimately familiar. Memories of something I have not experienced directly. Memories I arrived with. Memories that crawled in and tucked up and live on within me.

It wasn't long I'd been standing there when I heard the young man walking the track that goes, more or less, from the mast down to a gate in the surrounding stone wall. I did not turn, but continued listening, waiting anxiously, I suppose, to hear the gate latch rise—because, as it turned out, I was not convinced that once he'd shut the gate behind him the young man would go right, and carry on back down the hill, away from me. I looked across to where some distant trees were black, and I looked at the mud and the rainwater that quaked minutely in the mud's depressions—there, directly, in front of my boots—then I stepped a little way forward so that my arms came down to rest along the top rail of the gate. So be it, I thought. Let him come this way. It might in fact be the very reason why you were drawn out of your house this evening. Wearing only your nightclothes beneath a long thin coat. It might, in fact, just be the very thing you need. Let him come this way. By this time I had no difficulty acknowledging that the alarm that had coincided with his appearance on the road had not been incited by fear of him but rather by the horror I had felt towards my own twisted longing. A horror which had now more or less receded, along with my fleshly reticence. It might just feel like the most natural thing in the world, I thought.

The black trees
The tilting sphere
The humid bovine nostril
The sprawling chandelier
The thin lace trim
My damp unbrushed hair

Claire-Louise Bennett

All of them fleetingly tangible co-ordinates in an immemorial network of force and transmutation, of which the twilit taking of me was perhaps the final and most vital collaborating element. It came to me, not for the first time—so in fact I was reminded— that the world is always looking. Always looking back at me, always watching me, always studying me, discerning how exactly I might be best put to use in the eternal effort to give shape and form to its immeasurable spectrum of ineffable ecstasies and sorrows. It is the same for everyone, more or less. Yes indeed, we are all called upon to become a function of this overarching and irresolvable hunger. Alas, despite the rampant signals, something somewhere went slack and nothing further was issued. The gate closed and the young man turned right and made his way back down the hill. Away from me, hands in pockets. There was then a feeling of abnegation, followed by a vertical sense of redundancy.

Vague sensations really, hardly mine at all. And whatever intensity there had been drifted off and the usual way of things resumed. I felt quite chilly in fact. The cows were still there by the gate as I walked by on my way down the hill. I slowed down a little and thought of Jesus, I don't know why. Perhaps you all think I'm Jesus, I said, and then looked over at the windows of a neighbouring house. A light came on. There were plants along the sill. Soon enough I was outside my own cottage, admiring its green door and deep-set windows. Fancy that, I thought. What a very lovely place to live. Then I arrived inside and after a few moments I went across to the desk and resumed looking through a book of photographs by Clarence H. White.

Morning, 1908

The Black Lark

after I Know Why The Caged Bird Sings *by Maya Angelou*

The breaking and entering
of an eight year old
in yellow afternoon sun
sudden as love or hate.
Scimitar sundering
through the eye of a needle
blinded by nothing
it could name.
The terrible redundancy
in his face
still shackling your tongue
long after slick-suited uncles
left him for dead.
Later lashing you.
Seeing sullenness in silence
sent you back
to a grandmother in Stamps.

You liked her store best at dawn
waiting in slatted light
to be opened
like a tabernacle or a heart.
Mute mornings strung
with pearls of promise
till doors unwrapped
the red dirt yard
you raked at night
drawing moons
and stars and solar winds
in Arkansas soil.

Cinnamon constellations
circling a chinaberry tree
pledging shade to barbers
with glinting scissors
scraping cut-throats
troubadours plucking juice harps
twanging cigar-box guitars
cotton pickers come
to buy canned sardines
sody crackers and peanut paddies.
You soundlessly serving
haloed in gold from a coal-oil lamp.

Layered nacreous shell shielding
that small sense of self
brittle body armour
polished the day
she came with a name
spilling apple blossom
and Queen Anne lace.
Teacher telling you
flat words flush
with page were half dead.
Reading poets old and new
aloud only for you
chamois voice coloured
azure and amethyst
each letter enweaved
syllables shelled words unfurled.
What could you say
when she asked you to speak?
Black lark rising from mother-of-pearl.

Clare McCotter

Six Months

There is no way to stretch six months of love
across fourscore and ten.

The decades shrug it off.

No way to weave the thinning threads to cosy up old age,
silk-sooth the brittle weft, the aging warp of joints.

You might eke out the days with sex,
pretend you've captured what escaped—
but still, the silent mornings take their toll.

You might dilute the last remaining drops
to spread across the years,
take what you will from childbirth, work and friends—
the quiet joys the mags all recommend.

But other kinds of love cannot come close—
cannot get near the mad muddied need
that sent you diving from a cliff top into silent waves,

cracking your skull against his granite chest.

Lou Wilford

Fine as Feathers
Tania Hershman

What do you want, he said. The way he looked at me. What do you want? He said it again as if maybe I hadn't heard.

    Cut short, I said.

    Pale skin, he said. Light brown hair.

    Cut short, I said. Fine as feathers.

    His face was an old oil painting, his eyes were from some other century. And there I was, like a house with its beams exposed. He put out a hand and although I understood the transaction, understood that this was part of how it had to be, I winced. He said nothing. Scissors in one hand, his other hand hovered.

    Fine as feathers, he said.

I think you will laugh at me, when I tell you about it. I think you'll go Freudian, talk about blades and skin and mutilation, sex and mother issues.

    A hair cut, you say.

    I felt, I say. I felt it had something more. He wasn't the usual. You know.

    Effeminate, you say, and smirk. You smirk as if you know all this better than I do.

    I didn't want to use that word, I say, and turn to look through the window into the street because you aren't being nice, and I need you to be nice. Because you have a cruelty in you that comes through when what I need is kindness.

He raised his scissors and I closed my eyes. As I sat there I heard a bird and the sound came closer. The bird was singing, and the motion of him cutting, of him severing the ends, fitted in with the bird's odd sounds. As if he and the bird were dancing and my hair was dancing with them. Even though my eyes were shut, I saw this bird, its great plumage, its red throat. I saw him turn to the bird, still cutting my hair. And then I was outside and looking in at myself. And then I was the bird.

You have very little difficulty interpreting the dream. I know you think you sound sympathetic. I know you think you sound a great many things.

You are full of fear, you say to me. You long for wings, you long for your chains to be cut.

You are smug.

But who is he? I say, looking at you, looking into you as if to beg for something more like me, something more familiar.

He's just a conduit, you say.

What if he's God, I say, and then I wish I hadn't, I want to stuff the words back in.

Your look then is everything. Your look peels back my skin and I know we will never make it through this.

I was the bird then, and you were in the chair. He looked to me as if he wanted me to say something, to make some sound. I knew what he wanted. I opened my beak and it poured forth, and it came from something so deep inside, a sort of singing speech and so he cut and cut and cut some more. And then, when he had shorn your head, he moved the scissors closer. Closer to your neck, that pale blue vein. And you, looking in the mirror, didn't see. You, admiring, had a wall which kept out all danger. I knew, when he turned to me again, that he was asking me. All I had to give was a sign. The tip of the blade, right by your neck. Metal on skin.

When the world ends

—Summer, 2008   (London, England)

Pig Thief

And the sun come up over the camp, a lump
rising in the throat.
The brook was cooking its small fish.
We pressed our feet to the cold-holding stones
like your grandmother fervently kissing her rosary.
It was Sunday.
You climbed on the waste pipe. We heard dirty water
like Chinese whispers
tell secrets to the depth of its python dark. It was holy.

                         Suddenly a bird! An Icarus!
Your lips open, a stone
split apart by the heat.
Take my hand and *run*!
to The Wasting Space.

Green places got their own gravity.
It's this that I miss the most.
Trees filter time as well as light. We'd make our slow
                      descent into the half-past five
                            like deep-sea divers,
                                    sinking.

I remember drinking the smell of it. Fox-
freighted, piss-
pungent, illicit like a cinema.
A scrum of stunted pines
behind the rec ground,
a reminder that once we'd been wild:

far as the tarmaced car park.
Far as the concrete overpass.
Far as the prison
and the road pointing *South*.

continues…

You come to me, Pig Thief.
Your hands flashed small
        and white
        and brazen
against the navy of my blazer.
Dowry of *shit-fucks*!
heaping the air between us.

                This is The Wasting Space. We will tell stories.

The sudden shelter of the trees
leaves a ringing in our ears,
an echo like the hollow crash of surf.

I slit your hand like the skin of an apple.
I slit your hand like the belly of a fish.
Mix with me, Pig Thief,
my blood's not bad but it's hungry.
It's drinking the hole in your hand.

Sometimes there's an autumn
of hairless women. Pages of porn
torn into shreds
of shiny thigh/grinning, goofy, custard-
pie/cum-shot faces/lips big
with blow-job collagen.

Plug up the holes in the ground/ staunch
nature/insect myriads/birds
mend the spiky
mess of their nests
with the loose leaves of wanked-on women.

                Mix with me, Pig Thief,
            our *together* is better than theirs.

They belong to us, these After Woods. We're fused
by the death-trap seam,
welded together like cut-and-shut cars.

Feel my head, Pig Thief!
I'm as hot as a county tyre fire!
Feel my heart! The thrum
of an electric razor! And my brain
is throbbing like a juicy bone. The buzz off of me,
like jellies and e! A hum!
I'm sloshing like an egg in a leaky radiator!

                The light pours out of me like Saint Theresa,
                        like an open fridge.

                These are The After Woods. We will tell stories.

We will wear water. We will have gardens and draw water. Our gardens will be made of stone.
We will catch the water in pink plastic tubs,
ripped out from remodelled bathrooms in show homes.
We will ride white horses over the rubble.
                          I'll be a fine lady.
                                When the world ends.

Fran Lock

Security

Before they changed the streetlights to orange
bedrooms were dark enough for ghosts
to mumble between floorboards
hungering for the toes of children.

On no-moon nights shadows slid
along alleyway walls,
while an ear-strain away on the path behind
                          footsteps tapped,
stars the only witness.

Before they changed the streetlights to orange
there were no mechanical eyes
clicking round the town square to spy on
the carnal abandon of teenagers.

Now city night skies burn vermilion
around the guttering moon,
and all you can see through the trespassing glare
is a pinpoint shiny satellite
                          watching you.

Nicola Griffin

I Can Do This
Colin Corrigan

There was a queue to check in his suitcase, a queue for security, a queue at the cigarette counter. There was a queue to get on the plane, even though Phil had forked out the five euro for priority boarding. A family of seven crowded into the seats in front, beside, and behind him, and spent the flight bickering and swapping places and being excited about air travel. Even the parents acted like it was their first time flying, like they had eaten too many sweets.

In Faro, he waited twenty minutes for his suitcase to come through the thick plastic flaps, and fifteen minutes at the lost luggage desk. He filled out three forms. As he was collecting the keys for his rental car, though, something reminded him that he was on holiday. Maybe it was the attendant's smile, or the way her shorts crept up the back of her thighs when she leant down to get his GPS, but as he walked towards the rental lot, with the shining black tarmac under his feet and all that blue sky overhead, he felt the stress of his life in Dublin push up through his skin and out into the warm morning air like so much sweat.

He was looking forward to seeing his wife.

Two hours later he was lounging by the pool of his villa, cold beer in hand. Palm trees lined the perimeter of the garden, their paradise-shaped shadows reaching across the terracotta tiles. Jack and Saoirse were in the water, throwing around the beach ball he'd picked up on his way from the airport. Stretched out on her pink lilo, Carol bopped on the surface of the pool to the music of their childrens' movements. Phil closed his eyes and felt the sun's opiate rays on the skin of his face and his chest, and he lay still on the lounger and listened to the water splashing, the birds singing, his own breathing.

'Will you cut it out!'

'It was Jack,' said Saoirse.

Carol rolled off her lilo and flopped into the water. She swam to the pool's edge near where Phil was sitting, and, inhaling sharply, pushed herself up out of the pool. Phil watched her bronzed cleavage lurch and swell over the rim of her indigo swimsuit and felt his dick wake up. Carol was still a beautiful woman, from certain angles. Patting her face and shoulders with a white towel, she came over and stood close to his chair. He ran his index finger up the inside of her knee, intercepting the drops of pool water running down her leg. She stepped back out of his reach and towelled her hair.

'Sandy asked us over for dinner tonight,' she said.

'Who's Sandy?'

'I told you about her. She's in my Portuguese class.'

'Are you still doing those?'

'You think I should have just quit?'

Phil took a mouthful from his beer.

'What does she do?'

'She's writing her doctoral thesis, on geochemistry or something. Please don't ask her about it, she can go on and on.'

'It has to be tonight?'

'Robert is going back to London in the morning.'

'Who's Robert?'

'Her husband, Phil. I told you.'

'I thought we'd have a quiet night in.'

She stopped drying her hair and looked at him.

'I mean, it's our first night together in nearly two months,' he said.

She resumed her towelling.

'It'll be fun, you'll like her. And Robert's a good laugh too.'

He drank another mouthful of beer.

'We'll bring the kids,' she said. 'We won't stay late.'

After he had put Jack and Saoirse to bed for a nap, Phil stepped out into the sun room. Carol was collecting toys off the floor and rearranging the cushions on the sofas, and he stood for a moment and watched her. She wore lemon shorts and a light blue tank top that stretched across her breasts and the folds of her midriff. Most of the weight she had gained had settled on her trunk; her arse and legs looked almost as they did before she'd had children. He walked up behind her and reached around to place his palm flat against her stomach. She sniffed loudly and wrinkled her nose.

'You'd better take a shower,' she said, and she picked up the pile of toys and left the room. He looked out through the floor to ceiling windows at the For Sale sign on the front lawn, and wondered how he hadn't noticed that on his way in.

Their en suite's shower was also a sauna with built-in hydromassage jets. Phil splashed more water on the electric coals and relaxed on the fold-down seat. Breathing in the hot, thick air, he remembered the first time he had sat there. It was back when Saoirse was a baby and Jack an element of their family plan. The shower had been installed a few weeks before, while he was still in Dublin, as his birthday present to Carol. He'd been ushered out of his car, and his clothes, into the steaming heat, and she had gone straight onto her knees and given him a blow job. Then he remembered another time, before they were married, when she had spent a winter studying in Milan. He had surprised her half way through the semester by showing up at her flat, and he had fucked her, doggy style, right there on the carpet just inside her front door.

Through the steamed-up glass, he saw Carol walk into the bathroom, and he slid open the shower door with his toe. She put a towel next to the sink, and said over her shoulder as she left:

'Don't be all night in there.'

Phil knocked off the sauna and turned on the water jets. He moved his back and shoulders against the force of the spray, kneading his tired muscles, and thought, I'm going to miss this. He stepped out onto the cool tiles and dried himself off with the towel, then wiped the mirror and squared up to his reflection. The Carpe Diem tattoo that he had inscribed on his twenty-two-year-old pec sagged down either side of his nipple, like a frown.

'I heard you got a new job.'

Phil looked up in surprise at Sandy, who was sitting across from his armchair on a giant bean bag. He wasn't expecting to have to talk about this.

'That's right,' he said.

'Congratulations!' She turned to Robert, who was leaning back into the couch, next to Carol. 'Phil got a position in AIB's repossessions department.'

Phil looked at Carol.

'It's a growth industry,' said Robert.

Phil nodded.

'The department's actually six times bigger than it was two years ago.'

'What were you in before?'

'Account management. Carol says you work in the City?'

'Bonds. Goldman Sachs. Went quiet there for a while but we've bounced back pretty strong.'

Phil nodded, and swirled the ice in his glass. Then he looked at Sandy.

'Carol tells me you're into geochemistry?'

'I told you not to ask about her thesis.'

Carol kicked her shoes into the corner of their room and began taking off her jewellery. Phil walked up to her back and unzipped her dress.

I Can Do This

'You look great tonight,' he said, easing the light fabric over the tanned skin of her shoulder. 'You're black.'

'I know,' she said, with what seemed like a wistful stare at her arm.

Phil rubbed his nose against her neck, then turned her around to kiss her on the lips. She didn't open her mouth, and after a couple of seconds she eased his hands off her hips, went into the en suite, and began brushing her teeth. Phil picked up his iPod and scrolled through the artists, going straight for Marvin Gaye. He lodged it on the sound system's dock, and as the room filled with the rich bass tones of *In Our Lifetime*, he draped himself across the bed. Carol came back from the bathroom and began setting the alarm clock.

'I made an appointment for Saoirse at the optician's in the morning.'

'Oh yeah?'

'She looks so confused when she squints. Her new teacher will get the wrong idea.'

'Sometimes she really is just confused.'

'Can you take her?'

'You want me to take her?'

She swung the hangers along the rail of her wardrobe, and chose a white T-shirt.

'I'm playing tennis with Helen.'

Phil propped himself up on his elbow. She shrugged.

'We play every Wednesday.'

'You arranged the appointment for the same morning as your tennis game?'

'It will give you a chance to spend time with the children.'

'I'm taking Jack as well, then? He'll want to get glasses too.'

'Can you put the music down a bit?'

Phil lay back onto his pillow and looked at the ceiling. He only had ten days to relax and enjoy the pool and the beaches and bars, and for the very last time, assuming they managed to find a buyer for the villa. Carol had been here with the kids for almost two months.

'How much is this going to cost?'

'Half what we'd pay in Dublin.'

'Could she not get them through the PRSI or something?'

Carol walked around to the sound system and lowered the volume.

'It hasn't come to that, has it?'

He held out his hand towards her. Ignoring it, she pulled back the sheet he was lying on top of and got underneath. With much pulling and tugging, he managed to squirm in beside her. He slid his body along the mattress and pressed himself against her side. He kissed her shoulder, her cheek, her neck. She lay still, and flinched a little when his lips reached her earlobe. He sighed and rolled back onto his pillow, and felt his blood flush up his neck and into his face. He counted back through the weeks to the last time they had sex. Eleven, he decided: seven since she'd been here, and another four before she left Dublin. He wanted to say something. He had no idea how to say it. Then he felt her shift her weight, and her hand reached down into his boxer shorts. He smiled and closed his eyes.

But then he wondered why she had changed her mind. Was she just humouring him? Did she feel sorry for him? He thought of her sitting close to Robert on his white leather couch, absorbed by his stories, laughing at his stupid jokes. Robert who was still pulling in a hundred grand a year plus bonuses. Then he remembered again that blow job in the shower, and he lifted his arm and rested his fingers on top of her head. She leant towards him and kissed his face, and began moving her hand a little faster. For some reason he thought of his suitcase, floating somewhere in that non-place between airports.

'What's wrong?'

'Nothing. Don't stop.'

He rolled onto his side, facing her, and reached down in the direction of her clitoris. At first she crossed her legs, but then in slow, smooth increments, opened them. She moaned softly in his ear, and he felt himself grow again in her hand. He pulled up her nightdress, and she lifted her hips off the mattress to let him slide off her knickers. Kicking away his boxer shorts, he crawled in between her knees and entered her. He smiled again, and concentrated on his dick and tried to control his breathing as they moved their hips in unison. His mind went back to her flat in Milan, and he remembered the heat of the carpet under his knees, the feel of her hair tight in his fist. Pulling out, he grabbed her calf with both hands and tried to roll her over onto her face.

'What are you…?'

He remembered the ease with which he used to swing her around. Planting his foot a little to the side, he pulled again at her leg, trying to steer her into position. After a moment she seemed to understand and rolled over and lay flat on her stomach. He wanted her up on her knees.

I can do this, he thought. He dug his fingers into each side of her waist and took a deep breath and heaved her midriff six inches off the mattress.

'What the…? Ow!'

She slipped out of his grip and fell back onto her stomach. He reached around her again, pushed his hands in under her hips, and gritted his teeth.

'I can do this,' he said.

The Stillest Horse

On a hot sunless coach one Friday
we passed a field in which there was standing
the world's stillest horse. This horse
was like a picture of a horse
in three dimensions; this one
was taking stillness seriously.
She had something to teach us all.
Last night I told my boyfriend
he was perfect, and I cried.
Whoever thought there was such a thing
as simple language? Only a still horse
makes stillness less complex.
Likewise a boyfriend much loved can simplify
somehow the idea of loving:
the conceptual denseness becoming at night
a close pack of white noise
and expressing itself wordless
in the small ragged o of mouth
or the full embodied trembling
which takes away thought.
We've let this way of love escape from language:
run away, little lovingness,
while you're still uncorrupted by words,
light out for the territory
now and take us sleeping with you.
At night to him I will whisper
that he is the still horse,
all embodiment of being,
the o of mouth,

and also that he is a true poet
and that if I could love him
without words more truly
and take all words out of thought
I would cut out my tongue.
Crying I will whisper this and he will sleeping
place a sleep-hand over me
because he doesn't need words to love,
being a true poet,
showing a true thing essentially wordless
and the words do not damage the thing shown:
he is true and loves in sleep also
and being loved by him, I too am asleep
asleep and silently communicating
love and feeling it languageless
an embodiment of one true feeling,
still.

Sally Rooney

The Waking

Those first few days every part of her wakened,
the seedling eyes stirred by sunlight, tight fists
clamped to her chest like a medieval knight
and slowly loosening, as if the metal hands
were reminded of their likeness to petals
by the flowing hours. Her colours, too,
rose up like disturbed oils in a lake, pooling
through the birth-tinge into human shades,
her ink eyes lightening to an ancestral blue.
The scurf and residue of me on her scalp floated
easily as a pollen from the sweet grass of her hair.
She reminded me of a fern, each morning more
unfurled, the frond-limbs edging away from her
heart, the wide leaves of her face spread to catch
my gaze. Once, I saw the white down of her skin
cloud in my hands, the cream ridges of her nails
drift like crescent moons. The thick blue rope
she had used to descend me tossed like a stone,
as though she was finally free.

Carolyn Jess-Cooke

Ostrich
John O'Donnell

By then there were nine of us left in the minibus. The others had got out at Portbane, with shouts of 'See you tomorrow,' and slaps on the side and the back doors. If we'd looked we could have seen them through the back window; we could have watched them walking away into the night, Sammy and Davy and Tommy and Harry T., the glow of Harry T.'s cigarette rising and falling as he limped alongside the others into the darkness. We could have said goodbye. But we didn't; we sat back, spreading ourselves into the spaces left and continued the banter we'd been at all the way home from Bests, and we were still at it as we came to the top of the hill when Stuey let one go. It was definitely Stuey; a small self-satisfied trumpet blast, the stink quickly filling the air inside. 'Jesus, Stuey,' said Steven, waving his hands theatrically to get rid of the smell. Others joined in, Billy and Gerald and Gordon and Harry O., all groaning and fanning the air. 'Open a window, Dickie,' said Johnnie. He'd worked longer in Bests than any of us, Johnnie, he was just about to retire. 'For Chrissakes, open a window.' Stuey just kept laughing and saying it wasn't him, though he knew we knew it was. Dickie wound the driver's window down half way, and as the January night air rushed in we all leaned forward, even Stuey, inhaling with exaggerated relief, and it was then we saw at the bottom of the hill the light in the middle of the road.

*

Stella says I never talk about it. But I do, I do talk about it; I just don't always want to talk about it when she wants to talk about it. Anyway, what's to talk about? He's gone. Talking won't bring him back.

*

The light swung back and forth as the minibus came closer; it was a torch, signalling to us to slow down. There were no other lights out here; the road was dark and very quiet. 'What's he doing out here at this hour?' said Dickie, half to himself as he crunched down through the gears and prepared to stop. 'Police,' said Harry O. But as we neared we could see it wasn't the police: it was a man dressed in black, with some kind of hood covering his face, except for two big holes cut out for the eyes. 'Drive on, drive on,' shouted Johnnie. But the minibus had almost stopped, the headlights lighting up the road and the hedges on either side, like a stage, and under the beam of the headlights the hedges seemed to dissolve as more and more figures emerged out onto the road, in front of us and beside us and behind us as well. Dickie was trying to get the minibus into gear again, to get it going, but already there was someone at the driver's door, trying to yank it open. There were others at the passenger's side and the back doors as well, pulling at the handles and banging and shouting. Harry O. tried to hold the inside handles shut but he couldn't. The back doors were flung open and there were four of them outside, pointing what looked like guns and screaming 'Get out, the lot of youse, get out.'

*

Sixteen years ago. Just around the time all this other stuff started. We'd bought a pram, a cot, lots of things; so that we'd be ready. He lived for four days. The doctor knew as soon as he was born that he wasn't going to make it. I saw him once, in the incubator. I don't know about these things, but he looked long, lying there; one of the nurses said he was going to be tall, like me. I liked that. I never cried once, though Stella couldn't stop crying. The hospital allowed her to stay in an extra day. On the last day I was sitting beside the bed while she was asleep, just looking at her, when the main doctor came in. The tie he was wearing had lots of golf balls on it. 'This one just wasn't meant to be,' he said. I couldn't think how to reply, so I just said 'Ach sure I know, doctor.' He looked at the chart at the end of the bed, and then at Stella; she was still asleep. 'Ye were lucky to have gotten as far as ye did,' he said. He shook my hand, and said goodbye, and then he left. I think I knew what he meant. Stella'd been four weeks short of full term when it happened. But it didn't feel like we'd been lucky.

*

We clambered out into the night and they were shoving us round the side between the minibus and the ditch until we got to the front. Johnnie and Dickie were already there, with two men either side of them. The engine was switched off but the headlights were still on, making Johnnie and Dickie look very pale; and I thought, Jesus, if someone doesn't start the engine the lights'll soon drain the battery right down, and then one of them—the Hood, I think—said, 'Right, which of youse is a Pape?'

*

One of the other doctors, a younger one, did say it would be good if we could talk about it. But who would you talk to about it anyway? Not the boys in Bests. There was enough going on in Bests anyhow. Morgan, the foreman, was a right bastard to our lot, though there were less and less of our crowd working there; just me, and O'Neill up in Orders, and McCollum in the wages office. But you wouldn't be talking to them, nor to the other lot either. The younger ones, Gordon and Harry O., would be sniggering as Morgan stomped red-faced up and down the factory floor bellowing about production numbers and how he could find plenty to replace us. 'He just doesn't like you, Ollie,' Gerald said in the canteen, looking at me with those big sad bloodhound eyes. 'You could come in here on a white horse wearing a Rangers jersey and an Orange sash shouting "Up King Billy," and "Fuck the Pope," and Morgan still wouldn't like you. It's nothing got to do with you not being a Prod.' I like Gerald. But I didn't talk to him about it either.

*

Gordon and Harry O. were shaking their heads as we all stood on the side of the road, while one of them, a boy no more than sixteen, though big enough all the same, walked up and down the line, stopping in front of each of us to shine a torch in our faces. Gerald was second last; I was last. As the torch came closer I felt Gerald tug my sleeve, once, quickly. 'Say nothing, say nothing,' he said. The boy came to Gerald and gave him a little shove as he jiggled the torch in his face. And then he came to me.

*

And sure who'd want to listen? Back when it happened, there were lots of people calling to the door. Eileen Leahy carried round a big pot of stew, and the Donohoe girls brought over plates of sandwiches and cakes, but no one mentioned it. Father McElhone said how sorry he was, and on the altar he'd gone on about God's will. But no one ever once asked, 'So Olly, how does it feel to have lost your baby, your son?' Only baby, as it happened. I think everyone was just afraid to talk about it. In McGeeney's shop there were shy nods from other customers, and old McGeeney came out from the storeroom to shake my hand and say it was 'a bad business.' The day after the funeral I went down to the Dew Drop Inn on my own, just to get out of the house. It was late afternoon and there was no one in the place except for Traps McFadden, sitting on his usual stool at the far end of the bar. Traps bred greyhounds and was a bit touched. I'd never spoken to him, but as soon as he saw me come in he saluted me, and beckoned me over. 'Sorry for your trouble,' he said hoarsely. 'But they're good stock, the O'Tierneys,' he continued. Stella's family. 'Sure, she'll whelp again.' 'Hush now, Traps,' said Brendan behind the bar, setting down a glass in front of Traps, 'don't be bothering the poor man.' I sat down at one of the tables. Brendan brought me over a whiskey but refused to accept any money, and went back in and sat up on a stool behind the counter in silence, drinking a mineral. Nobody said anything. Sure what was the point? Talking wasn't going to solve anything.

*

I could smell the beer off him. But there was something else, another smell; the smell of chips. That smell I remembered, nights outside the takeaway when I first started out with Stella; the two of us with a skinful on board, each holding a warm bag of chips, the vinegar slathered on and already beginning to stain the bag in patches, and the salt glistening like little snowflakes on the golden chunks as we ate them, Stella and me. Sometime this evening, before he'd hidden in the hedges on the side of this road, waiting, this boy had got his hands on some beer, and then he'd had chips. The torch he was carrying wasn't really a torch; it was a bicycle lamp and he was shining it in my eyes. The he turned to the Hood, the light still jiggling over my face. 'This one here,' he said, his voice rising in excitement. 'The big lanky fella. This here's one.'

*

The last time it had been mentioned, we were sitting on the couch, watching telly. The news was showing a funeral; more than one, actually, there were three of them. They were carrying them in to the graveyard, coffin after coffin, like they were coming off an assembly line. 'Why do you never go?' she asked. 'Go where?' I said. 'You know where,' she said. 'The grave. James's grave.' James had been Stella's father's name. The cameras were showing the crowds around the opened ground, crying and sighing and dabbing at their eyes. 'Ach, don't start this again,' I said. 'But you don't,' she said. 'Like an ostrich, so you are, Ollie, with your head stuck in the sand.' She was shouting now. 'A big ostrich, that's what you are.' I didn't say anything. The telly showed the priest saying some prayers, and then it was back to the newsreader, who was talking in front of a picture of a building that had been blown apart earlier that day. A minute or two later she got up from the couch and went out of the room. I could hear her clattering around with the kettle and the teapot in the kitchen, and I knew she was crying.

*

How did this boy know me, know who I was? There must have been a moment when he'd seen me. In McGeeney's, perhaps. Or the Dew Drop Inn, he could have been there one evening when I'd been there. Maybe he'd been waiting anxiously at the counter, hoping to be served. But how did he know? Unless he'd seen me outside St Mary's, in the carpark, after Mass. I don't remember ever seeing him before, anywhere. Maybe he worked in Bests once, though I don't think so. But he knew me somehow, knew me well enough to know. The Hood came over to me, and I could hear shouting as he grabbed me and dragged me back down behind the minibus; Gerald's voice. 'Leave him be,' he was saying. Dickie was shouting too; 'It's alright, he's one of us!' Gordon and Harry O. said nothing. 'Right,' said the Hood. He adjusted something on his gun; there was a little click. He stepped slightly away from me, as if to get a better angle. There were still two of them standing on either side of me, but when he motioned to them they stood apart. 'Right,' he said again. 'Now get you down that road, and don't look back.'

*

She's wrong. I did go, once, about two months after he died. Outside the gate a man was selling flowers, and just inside the entrance there was a woman in a little hut who asked my name and directed me, though it still took me a while to find the grave again. There were flowers there from the last time Stella'd been, laid carefully at the foot of the little headstone that gave his name and the date when he was born, and the other date, days later, when he'd died, and then underneath the words *With The Angels Once More* that Stella had wanted. I knelt down by the grave and started to say a little prayer, and then I stopped. None of this prayer stuff would make any sense to him, I thought. So instead I just said his name. 'Well, James', I said, 'you poor wee fella'. I could feel my eyes starting to well up. 'You poor wee mite', I said. A woman at a grave a few rows down glanced over at me and then turned away. I stood up and headed for the entrance. And I never told Stella. I don't know why I didn't tell her, but I didn't.

*

I started running away from the minibus into the darkness. I could hear gunfire. Any moment now, I thought, one of these will hit me. The shots kept coming, little muted whipcracks. But there was another sound as well I could hear, over the sound of the gunshots and the sound of my shoes slapping the tarmac as I ran; it was the sound of men screaming, crying out in pain. I kept running, though. I didn't dare turn round to see what was happening in the dip of the road that was still lit up by the headlights of the minibus. I kept running on my big long ostrich legs, and I never looked back.

August 30, 2012

desire's cost is soil soil soil
the house mirrored by a house house
buddleia cut down   bees fizz fizz
a robin red breast flits and flies
where is my nest was that my nest
a cat rakes through the new soil
mine is this mine territory mine
this is your life fleeting who needs money
or a father who stays on the island
who needs what no more kids so
a radio plays or is it the jingle of the TV news
TV
familiar childhood darkness
your mother is cleaning and cleaning and
cleaning and cleaning
international disappeared day
clean
what—everywhere in Ireland it's no seasons
seven remain the technology is there
a little bit of courage is all that's
have to keep on hoping
breath in my body keep asking
disappeared people people who know
who know where he is
nine of the disappeared won't give up
and so my mother is weeping and
and my brother wants a lift
lift lift home

he talks talks talks talks to himself
and says says says Ireland is an everywhere and
the heart heart heart is a rotten fruit and
we played at sticks as kids
and
we played at sticks as kids
and we moved moved moved moved moved
remember that house where we were happy
happy happy then ran away yes yes yes remember it well
the pain has grown like an unwatered plant
changing growing into and out of the soil
where desire's cost is a farewell where one man
is talking talking talking talking talking
to the wind wind wind wind wind
to the water water water water water
to the hah hah hah
hah hah hah
to the hah hah
hah hah

Paul Perry

The Night of the Silver Fox
Danielle McLaughlin

They stopped for diesel at a filling station outside Longford town. It was late evening, dusk closing like a fist around two pumps set in a patch of rough concrete and a row of leafless poplars that bordered the forecourt. Kavanagh swung down out of the cab and slapped the flank of the lorry as if it were an animal. He was a red-faced, stocky man in his late thirties. As a child he had been nicknamed Curley because of his corkscrew hair and the name had stuck, even though he was now almost entirely bald, just a patch of soft fuzz above each ear.

There was a shop with faded HB posters in the window and boxes of cornflakes on display alongside tubs of Swarfega and rat pellets. 'Fill her up,' Kavanagh said to the teenager who appeared in the doorway. Then he spat on the ground and walked around the back of the building to the toilet.

Gerard stayed in the cab and watched the boy, who was about his own age, pump the diesel. The boy was standing well back from the lorry, one hand holding the nozzle, the other clamped over his nose and mouth. When his eyes met Gerard's in the wing mirror, Gerard looked away.

Three months in and he was still not used to the smell. The fish heads with their dull, glassy eyes; the skin and scales that stuck to his fingers; the red and purple guttings that slipped from the fishes' bellies. The smell of dead fish rose, ghost-like, from the meal that poured into the factory silos. Gerard shaved his hair tight, cut his nails so short his fingers bled. At night in the pubs in Castletownbere, he imagined fine shards of fish bone lodged like shrapnel beneath his skin and tiny particles of scales hanging in the air like dust motes. The smell didn't bother Kavanagh, but then Kavanagh had been reared to it.

'Daylight robbery,' Kavanagh said when he returned to the lorry. He handed the pump attendant the money. 'Bring me out two packets of Tayto and have a packet for yourself.' He shook his head as he climbed back into the cab. 'Daylight robbery,' he said again, 'four cent a litre dearer than Slattery's.'

Gerard didn't ask why they hadn't gone to Slattery's. Slattery's had stopped their tab a few weeks back and Kavanagh had been keeping his distance since.

Kavanagh hummed tunelessly while he waited for the boy to return with the crisps and his change. It was a fragment of a ballad he had taken up some time after they passed Gurrane, forty miles earlier, and he had not let it go since. Taped to the walls of the cab were pictures torn from magazines of women in an assortment of poses. They were mostly Asian and in varying states of undress: Kavanagh had a thing for Asian women. A photograph of Kavanagh's wife, Nora, taken at last year's GAA dinner dance, was stuck between a topless girl on a Harley Davidson and two dark eyed women in crotchless panties. Nora had blonde wispy hair and glasses and the straps of her dress dug furrows in her plump shoulders.

'We're in injun territory now,' Kavanagh said, when he saw the boy coming across the forecourt, 'these Longford bastards would rob the teeth out of your head,' and he counted the change down to the last cent before putting it in his pocket.

It was almost dark when they pulled back onto the road. Kavanagh threw a packet of crisps across the cab. 'That'll keep you going,' he said, 'we can't count on Liddy for grub.' Four miles before Kilcroghan, they turned down a narrow side road, grass growing up the centre. Briars tore at the sides of the lorry. 'There's a man in Dundalk runs one of these on vegetable oil,' Kavanagh said. 'Did you ever hear anything about that?'

'No,' said Gerard, although he remembered reading something in a newspaper a couple of months back. If he let on that he knew anything at all, Kavanagh would have him tormented. Kavanagh had a child's wonder for the new and the strange. Each new fact was seized upon and dismantled, taken apart like an engine and studied in its various components. He had been bright at school but had left at fourteen to work in the fish factory.

Kavanagh shook his head. 'I don't think I could stand it,' he said. 'The smell. It must be like driving around in a fucking chipper.' Gerard glanced across at Kavanagh and tried to work out if he was serious. Kavanagh was watching the road, fingers drumming the steering wheel, humming to himself again. The light from the dashboard lent a vaguely sainted glow to his features. Gerard decided not to say anything. Kavanagh broke off his humming and sighed. 'You're all chat this evening,' he said, 'I can't get a word in edgeways. Are you in love or what?'

'Fuck off,' Gerard said but he was smiling as he turned to look out at the trees that reached black and tall from the hedges, their branches slapping against the lorry's window.

Gerard had first been to Liddy's mink farm back in August, six weeks after he started working for Kavanagh. He had not been able to shake the memory of the place since. It was partly the farm itself and it was partly Liddy's daughter. She was about seventeen with blue-black hair and a nose stud, eyes heavily ringed with black liner.

When Kavanagh had gone inside with her father, she had taken Gerard across the yard to show him the mink.

The mink were housed in sheds a couple of hundred feet long, twenty or thirty feet wide, with low, sloping roofs of galvanised sheeting. The sides were open to the elements, wind blowing in from the mountains to the west. Gerard followed the girl into the first shed and along a sawdust path down the centre. In wire mesh cages on either side were thousands of mink, mostly all white, with here and there a brown one. They darted back and forth and stood on their hind legs, heads weaving, snouts pressed against the wire. Their eyes glittered like wet beads, and they twisted and looped, twisted and looped, hurling their bodies against the sides of the cages.

Gerard stood in front of a cage and poked a finger through the mesh. A mink stopped chewing its fur and looked at him, a vicious tilt to its chin. It sniffed the air, crept closer and snapped, grazing the tip of his finger. Then it backed away to stare at him from a distance.

The girl was a couple of paces ahead, watching. 'I suppose you think it's cruel,' she said. Her hair was tucked into the hood of her jacket.

Gerard examined his finger and shrugged. 'It's none of my business,' he said.

The girl stared at him for a moment, saying nothing, her dark eyes narrowing. Then she sighed. 'It's what they're bred for,' she said, turning away, 'they don't know any different.'

It was dark when Kavanagh swung the lorry through a muddy entrance with rough concrete pillars on either side. The lorry lurched along an uneven track lined with chain-link fencing. In the distance, Gerard could make out the long, dark lines of the mink sheds, moonlight glinting on the metal roofs, and beyond them a huddle of outbuildings. 'Liddy hasn't paid since June,' Kavanagh said, 'so he'll need to come up with the cash tonight. I'll sort you out then.'

'It's alright,' Gerard said, 'it's grand,' although it wasn't all right anymore. Kavanagh hadn't paid him in three weeks and on his last visit home Gerard had to borrow from his father to pay the rent. 'I'll sort you out,' Kavanagh repeated as the lorry turned into the yard.

The farmhouse was a square two-storey building, its whitewash fading, weeds growing from crevices in the front steps. A cat ran across the lorry's path and hid behind a row of tar barrels. Liddy's mud-spattered jeep was parked in the yard, a back light broken. 'It would be easy to feel sorry for Liddy,' Kavanagh said, 'but what would be the use in that?' and they both got out of the lorry.

A light came on in the porch and Liddy himself appeared. He was a stooped, wiry man, a grey cardigan hanging loose from his shoulders, and his eyes darted from Kavanagh to Gerard and back again as he came towards them across the yard. His skin had the waxy, pinched look of a museum doll. It reminded Gerard of how his mother had looked in the months before she died and he knew immediately that Liddy was sick.

Danielle McLaughlin

'How're the men?' Liddy held out a bony hand to Kavanagh who took it in his own vast paw and squeezed until Gerard expected to hear bones crack. Liddy's daughter had come out into the porch. She was slouched against the door frame, arms folded, her black hair pulled loosely into a ponytail.

Liddy looked up at the night sky with its shifting mass of cloud. 'The rain will be on soon,' he said, 'you might as well get her unloaded. I'll put the kettle on for tea.'

Gerard went to release the back of the lorry but Kavanagh held up a hand. 'Hold on a minute,' he said, 'if it was tea I was after I could have stayed at home. Tea is fuck all use to me.'

The girl, wearing tracksuit bottoms and a vest, was coming down the porch steps and across the yard. She had the same black-ringed eyes that Gerard remembered from before.

Liddy had already begun to shuffle towards the house. He called back over his shoulder to Kavanagh. 'Don't you know I'm good for it?' he said, 'have I ever let you down yet?'

Kavanagh didn't budge. 'That's three loads you owe me now,' he said. 'I've bills to pay. I've this young fellow here to pay.' He nodded at Gerard who stood waiting by the lorry.

Liddy stopped. He gave a wheeze that shook his chest and caused him to bend almost double, hands on his knees. 'Sure what could a young lad like that want?' he said, when he righted himself again, 'a young lad like that would be happy sitting under a bush with a can.' He laughed then but Kavanagh didn't.

'Leave it for the time being.' It was the girl, her voice slightly muzzy as if she had been sleeping. She raised both hands behind her head and stretched like a cat. 'We can talk about it inside.' She turned and walked towards the house and the three men followed.

The porch was stacked with bags of coal and kindling. A plastic bucket and a yard brush stood in one corner, beside two pairs of wellington boots, caked with mud and sawdust. A picture of Pope John Paul II, arms outstretched, hung next to a calendar from the Fortrush Fisherman's Co-op, two years out of date, days circled and crossed in spidery ink. Beyond the porch was a dark, narrow hallway. Liddy faltered but the girl pushed open a door into a small sitting room.

There was a mahogany chest of drawers with ornate carvings that must have come from a bigger, grander house. Squares of faded linen were folded on top, next to a family of blue china elephants. The room smelled of things put away, of dust laid down on dust. The carpet was brown with an orange fleck and along one wall was a sofa in a dull mustard colour. On either side of the fireplace were two matching armchairs, their plastic covers still in place. A copy of the *Fur Farmers Yearbook* and a few tatty paperbacks sat on a coffee table.

Liddy took one armchair, Kavanagh the other. As he lowered himself onto the sofa,

Gerard caught a glimpse of himself in a mirror above the fireplace. His skin was still lightly tanned from days spent on the pier over the summer. His shorn hair carried a hint of menace to which he had not yet grown accustomed. He took off his jacket and placed it beside him on the sofa, and as he did so, thought that he caught a faint odour of dead fish. Through the open curtains, he saw the moon reflecting in the puddles that lay like small lakes upon the surface of the yard.

'You'll have a drop of something?' The girl spoke like a woman twice her age. Standing there, waiting for an answer, she could have been the woman, not just of the house, but of the farm and the yard, the dark rows of mink sheds and the wet fields and ditches out beyond.

Kavanagh shook his head. 'Tea's grand,' he said.

Her eyes settled next on Gerard who felt his face grow red.

Kavanagh looked across and chuckled. 'He's the strong, silent type,' he said, 'he has the women of Castletownbere driven half mad.' He winked at the girl. 'You could do worse.'

The girl, momentarily shy, gazed at the carpet and tucked a wisp of hair behind one ear. 'Tea's fine,' Gerard said and the girl smiled at him before going out of the room.

After she had gone, the men sat in silence. Kavanagh was never short of something to say and Gerard knew the silence was a shot across the bows: Kavanagh's way of sending a message to Liddy.

Liddy stared into the empty grate for a while and then, when there was still nothing from Kavanagh, he addressed himself instead to Gerard. 'What part of the country are you from yourself?' he said, 'and through what misfortune did you end up with this latchico?'

Gerard was a second cousin of Kavanagh's on his mother's side and Kavanagh had taken him on at the fish factory after he finished school that summer. It was partly Kavanagh's way of looking out for the boy after the death of Gerard's mother the year before. It was also because Gerard's father had lent Kavanagh the money to fix the factory roof after the storms the previous winter and Kavanagh had yet to repay him.

Gerard could feel Liddy's eyes on him, waiting for an answer. He was saved by Kavanagh breaking his silence. 'Isn't he the lucky boy to have a job at all?' he said. 'Every other lad his age is over in Australia.'

'Luck is a two-faced whore,' Liddy said, 'there's people said I was lucky when I got this place.'

Kavanagh fell quiet and when he spoke again it was to enquire after a relative of Liddy's who was in the hospital at Mount Carmel. The talk turned next to football and greyhounds and, for a while, a peace of sorts settled on the room.

When the girl came back with the tea she had changed into a low-cut pink top and a short black skirt that clung to her hips and thighs. Her hair, freshly brushed and more

Danielle McLaughlin

indigo than black, hung past her shoulders. She was carrying a tray with the tea and a plate of Club Milks and as she set it down on the coffee table, Gerard's eyes went to her plump, white breasts and slid into the valley between them. The girl was putting cups in saucers, pouring tea. Without warning she raised her head and caught him looking. She stared at him until, blushing, he returned the stare and he noticed for the first time that her eyes, which he had thought were brown, were in fact a very dark blue, almost navy. Then she straightened up, tucked the empty tray under her arm, and went out of the room.

Kavanagh unwrapped a Club Milk, took half of it into his mouth in one bite and chewed slowly. 'Well Liddy,' he said, 'what have you got for me?'

When Liddy leaned forward in his chair, his collar bones jutted like scythes through the thin wool of his cardigan. 'We had the activists a while back,' he said, 'Ten minutes with a wire cutters and I'm down a thousand mink. Next morning, I've a farmer at my door with a trailer full of dead lambs, all with holes in their throats.' Liddy shook his head and brought a hand to his own thin throat.

'Those fuckers should be shot,' Kavanagh said, 'Thundering bastards. I know what I'd do with their wire cutters.'

Liddy's hand left his throat and settled instead on his knee which immediately began to jig. 'We had a cull last month: Aleutian disease.'

Kavanagh sighed and put his cup down heavily on the table. 'Listen,' he said, 'Do I look like Mother Teresa? There isn't any of us has it easy.'

'If I'd known what I was letting myself in for,' Liddy said, 'I'd never have come out here.' He seemed to be talking more to himself than to Kavanagh. 'I'd have stayed in the city and saved myself a lot of trouble.'

'Trouble knows its way around,' Kavanagh said. 'I've the bank on my case, I've the wife on my case, and I've this young fellow here to pay.' He pointed to the pile of Club Milk wrappers that had accumulated in front of Gerard. 'Look at him, he's half-starved.'

Apart from the crisps in the lorry earlier, Gerard hadn't eaten anything since they left Castletownbere shortly after four o' clock. He was about to open another Club-Milk but now he put it back on the plate.

'I'll have it in a lump sum next time,' Liddy said.

'You'll have it tonight, or I'll turn that lorry around and drive back the way I came.'

'I've a man coming for pelts on Tuesday. Call in the next time you're passing.'

A flush was edging up Kavanagh's neck, spreading over his cheeks. 'There's nothing for nothing in this world,' he said. 'You can pay me tonight or you can go to hell.'

'I wouldn't have to go far,' Liddy said, 'look around you.'

A sullenness had come over Liddy. The forced banter of earlier had disappeared and in its place was a sour obstinacy that hardened into bitter lines around his mouth. Gerard had a sudden vision of how Liddy would look laid out: his body sunken in a too big suit, a tie awkward at his throat, even the silk lining of the coffin pressing heavy on his arms.

There was a noise outside in the yard; the clank of metal on concrete. Kavanagh was first on his feet, the others following behind. The girl was on a forklift. She wore no helmet and the wind that blew across the yard snatched at her hair, snaking it in black tails about her face. She had released the back of the lorry and was unloading a pallet of fish meal.

Kavanagh crossed the yard like a bull. The girl stopped the forklift but didn't get out. Her face was pale in the light of the porch lamp. 'Fucking cunt,' Kavanagh was roaring and he started to swing bags of meal from the forklift like they were candyfloss. Liddy watched from a distance. Gerard went to help but the girl had been intercepted early and already everything was back on the lorry. 'I thought I'd make a start,' she said. 'It's getting late.'

'Do you think I'm some class of fool?' Kavanagh said.

The girl's voice was soft, measured, as if calming a small child. 'You're no fool, Curley,' she said. 'Come here and talk to me.' She patted the passenger seat of the forklift. Kavanagh looked away and shook his head. 'I've enough time wasted,' he said, and began to walk towards the lorry.

The girl called after him. 'Hey, Curley,' she said, 'don't be like that.' Her voice dropped lower. 'You can't go yet, you haven't seen the silver foxes.' She was leaning out of the forklift, her shadow stretching across the yard. 'We brought them over from England last month. They're still only cubs.' She was looking directly at Kavanagh, her head tilted slightly to one side, her lips parted. 'Come down to the shed and I'll show you. You've never seen foxes like these.'

Kavanagh had reached the door of the cab. He stopped, one foot on the step. In the forklift, the girl patted the passenger seat again and winked. Kavanagh appeared to be considering. Liddy was standing by himself, staring at the ground. For a while everything was very still and there was only the sound of the wind rattling across the roofs of the mink sheds and the cry of a small animal in the trees beyond. Then Kavanagh strode across the yard to the forklift and climbed in. They drove off, the girl at the wheel, the wind whipping up her dark hair, Kavanagh bald and stocky in the seat beside her. The forklift went to the far end of the yard and disappeared behind some outbuildings.

Gerard and Liddy were left standing in the yard. Liddy looked like a man who had been struck. He did nothing for a moment, then turned and began his stooped walk back to the house. Gerard was about to go to the lorry and wait when Liddy shouted to him from the porch. 'You might as well come in,' he said.

This time, instead of going into the sitting room, they continued down the hall and into a small wood-panelled kitchen. A table and two chairs were pushed tight against one wall, a cooker, a sink, and an assortment of mismatched kitchen units against another. There was a wooden dresser stacked with old newspapers and chipped crockery. The stale grease of a fry hung in the air. To one side of the back door, in a glass display cabinet, was a stuffed brown mink. It was mounted on a marble base, which had an inscription that Gerard could not read. The mink stood on its hind legs, teeth bared in a rigid grin, front legs clawing the air.

Liddy took a bottle of whiskey from a cupboard beneath the sink and wiped two glasses on the end of his cardigan. He sat at the table and gestured at Gerard to sit beside him.

'She's gone five years now,' Liddy said, pouring the whiskey. Gerard didn't understand at first. He had been thinking of the girl behind the outbuildings with Kavanagh. The white breasts, the dark eyes. Her mouth, wide and loose; her red lips and the stud on her tongue that had flashed silver when she smiled at something earlier in the evening. Then he realised Liddy was staring at a photograph high on the wall above the dresser. It was of a woman, tall and angular, with straight brown hair, her hand resting on the shoulder of a girl in a First Holy Communion dress. 'I'm sorry,' Gerard said because he couldn't think of anything else to say and it was what people had said when his mother died.

'Oh, I'm not sorry,' Liddy said, throwing back his whiskey and pouring another, 'there's a lot I'm sorry about, but not that.' His weariness had been replaced with anger. 'She took herself off to Belfast. She told me she was going to stay with her sister but you can be sure she had a man waiting. It was always the same with that woman: she'd tell you that day was night.' His head jutted forward and Gerard smelled the sourness of his breath. 'I asked her to take the girl with her,' Liddy said, 'but she wouldn't.' He put down his glass and spread his hands wide, palms upwards, in supplication. 'What sort of life is it for a young girl out here? I asked her, but she left us to it, Rosie and myself.'

Rosie. The girl's name didn't suit her, Gerard thought. It was too tame, too domesticated. It was a name for a spoilt poodle in a wicker basket, not a girl with a tongue piercing who could drive a forklift. Liddy drank more whiskey. 'Rosie was twelve when she left,' he said, 'and what did I know about raising a child? A girl needs her mother. Boys are different, boys can make their way, but girls need mothers.'

Liddy fell silent, swirled whiskey around the end of his glass. Gerard wanted to get up and leave but knew that he could not. It was a moment before Liddy spoke again. 'It was coming out here did it,' he said. 'She was always a flighty woman. She had one eye on the door from the day I married her, but we got along well enough up to that. A couple of winters here and nothing could hold her.'

Liddy was becoming more and more agitated, his hands moving incessantly, almost knocking over his glass. Gerard's own glass was barely touched. He thought of Kavanagh and the girl in the shadows of the outbuildings. He wondered if silver foxes were the same as ordinary foxes, only silver, or if they were some different creature entirely, and then he wondered if there were any silver foxes at all. He imagined the cubs in Kavanagh's rough hands and Kavanagh, awed and silent, turning them this way and that.

'Her mother, bitch and all that she is, would make a better hand of her,' Liddy said, 'Rosie's a good girl, a fighter, but what chance has a girl out here?'

Gerard knew that he should say something but had no idea what.

'Rosie will be okay,' he said, 'Rosie's a smart girl.'

Liddy stared at him, his eyes bloodshot. All of the anger left him and he sagged over the table. 'She is,' he said, 'she's a smart girl. And a good girl.'

He set his glass down on the table and buried his head in his arms. The kitchen was utterly quiet, nothing but the sound of the wind whistling under the back door. A strange sound came from Liddy, half cough, half sob. Then another that caught and lengthened until it became a wail. Liddy was crying, his shoulders quivering, the top of his head shaking. Gerard took a mouthful of whiskey, felt it burn the pit of his stomach. Liddy was bawling now, his head still in his arms. Gerard pushed his chair back and stood up. He went over to the sink and placed his glass on the draining board. He took one last look at Liddy crumpled over the table, then left the kitchen and went back down the narrow hall and outside to the yard.

When he got to the lorry he discovered that Kavanagh had locked it and taken the key. The night had grown colder. Gerard remembered his jacket, still in the sitting room where he had left it earlier, but thought of Liddy weeping inside the house and decided to do without. A light was on in a prefab but the door, when he tried it, was padlocked and he took shelter instead beneath the overhang of its roof, next to a row of barrels. He wrapped his arms around himself and hoped that Kavanagh would not be long. Something warm brushed against his legs and he saw a cat dart from behind a barrel and streak across the yard.

He pressed his face against the prefab window. The walls were hung with pelts: thousands of headless, bodiless furs, their arms spread wide and pinned to wooden racks. On a bench was a machine with long silver-toothed blades and beside it, a pile of dead mink. He noticed a smell coming from the barrel nearest him and lifted the lid. Inside were the skinned corpses of the mink, pink and slippery and hairless. Gerard remembered a day in the woods near his home when he was a small boy. He had found a bald, half-formed baby bird beneath a tree, the egg shattered on the ground beside it, and had slipped it into his pocket, all dead and grey and slithery, to take home to his mother. He dropped the lid of the barrel and stepped back from the window.

The wind carried fragments of laughter up the yard and he saw Kavanagh and the girl returning on the forklift. This time Kavanagh was driving, the girl beside him, an arm flung across his shoulder. They slowed as they passed the pelt shed and waved. Gerard stepped out from the shelter of the building and walked behind the forklift to the lorry. A drizzle blew in from the mountains, stinging his face. Kavanagh, pink and sweating, jumped out of the forklift. 'Give us a hand,' he said to Gerard without looking at him and together they began to unload the lorry. Gerard shivered in his shirtsleeves but the cold, like the smell, didn't seem to bother Kavanagh.

Gerard felt someone touch his arm. The girl was behind him, holding his jacket. She didn't say a word but Gerard held out his arms and allowed her to slip the jacket on, let her zip it up and smooth it down over his shoulders.

Afterwards, as they turned the lorry in the yard, Gerard noticed Liddy standing alone in the porch. Gerard raised a hand and waved but Liddy didn't wave back. The girl was by the forklift, hands in her pockets. Gerard watched her in the rear-view mirror as the lorry drove out of the yard, saw her turn and walk towards the house, saw the light go out in the porch.

Kavanagh didn't speak until they reached the end of the muddy track and were back on the road. 'I'm calling on Clancy tomorrow,' he said, 'He owes me a few bob. I'll sort you out then.'

'It's alright,' Gerard said.

They drove in silence for a while, the only sound the relentless squeak of the wipers as the rain grew heavier. 'Tell me,' Kavanagh said, 'did you ever see a silver fox?' Gerard shook his head. Kavanagh let out a low whistle. 'Beautiful animals,' he said, 'beautiful. But why do you think their fur is that colour? Aren't they foxes at the end of the day?'

Gerard shrugged and looked out the window. Kavanagh kept talking, his voice becoming more animated, his hands restless on the steering wheel. 'They weren't silver exactly,' he said. 'You'd be expecting silver but it was more…' He paused and his eyes scanned the cab—his wife's photograph, the pictures of the Asian women, the collection of knick knacks on the dash. When his surroundings failed him, he clicked his tongue in exasperation. 'They were a sort of bluey-black,' he said, 'white bits on their tails and faces. Little balls of fur.' He went suddenly quiet, as if he had embarrassed himself.

Back on the main road, the lorry picked up speed as they headed south. A few miles on, Kavanagh spoke again. 'What kind of life is it at all?' he said, 'weaned at six weeks and shipped off in a crate?'

It was cold in the cab and Gerard pulled his jacket tighter around him. He put a hand to the inside pocket, felt for his wallet and realised that it was gone. Shadowy trees and ditches blurred past. The wind blew dark, shapeless things across the path of the lorry, things that might have been alive or might have been dead: tiny night creatures and flurries of fallen leaves. They drove on through small, half-lit towns, through dark countryside whose only light was the flicker of wide-screen televisions in bungalow windows. Kavanagh began to hum. It was the chorus of a country and western song, full of love and violence, and he kept it up until they reached Bantry and took the dark coast road for Castletownbere.

2013 SUBMISSION GUIDELINES

During 2013 *The Stinging Fly* will accept submissions in February, June and October. Submissions received in February 2013 will be considered for our October issue (Winter 2013–14); June 2013 submissions will be read for our Spring 2014 issue; October 2013 submissions will be read for our Summer 2014 issue.

We welcome submissions from Irish and international writers. All work submitted must be previously unpublished and ideally should not be under consideration elsewhere.

The postal address for submissions is: The Stinging Fly, PO Box 6016, Dublin 1, Ireland. We do not accept e-mail submissions.

Each submission should include an e-mail address for reply.

All submissions should be accompanied by a cover letter, which should include:

* Author's Name
* E-mail address and postal address
* Date of Submission
* Name of story/poems submitted
* Brief biographical note, if you wish.

Anyone submitting fiction and poetry should include separate a cover letter with each. All fiction submissions should be printed using 1.5 or double line spacing. Minimum font size: 11pt. Print on one side of the page only. Every piece of work should have the author's name printed or signed on it.

* No more than **one** story and/or **four** poems should be submitted during any one submission period.
* Short stories and poems should always be just as long (or as short) as they need to be.
* All submissions are read. The editors' decision may not be correct but it is final.
* With a limited budget, we are only in a position to offer contributors a discretionary token payment. They also receive two copies of the issue in which their work is featured and can order further copies at a discounted rate.
* Copyright remains in all cases with the author. Some work published in the magazine may also be included on our website.

Our Featured Poets

In each issue we publish a number of poems by a poet who is working towards a first collection. In 2013 we will only accept submissions for the Featured Poet slot during the **February** submission period. To be considered, please send us 6-10 previously unpublished poems. If we want to see more, we will get back to you.

Comhchealg

Is í 'Comhchealg' cuid Ghaeilge *The Stinging Fly*. Cuirtear fáilte roimh phíosaí Gaeilge ó scríbhneoirí úra. Is nós linn aistriúcháin Bhéarla a chur ar fáil i gcás na ndánta a roghnaítear. Chuige sin, déanaimid filí Béarla a chur ag obair ar shaothar a gcomhúdar. Leantar na treoirlínte iarratais thuas a bhaineann le filíocht Bhéarla.

THE STINGING FLY REVIEWS

The Ash and the Oak and the Wild Cherry Tree
by **Kerry Hardie** (The Gallery Press, 2012, €11.95)
Fireflies
by **Frank Ormsby** (Carcanet, 2009, £9.95)

In 'Sixty', the first poem of her new collection, Kerry Hardie sets the tone: ruminative, plaintive, a considered gravitas to every line:

> Everyone is slowly going home.
> The shadow of the pine
> lies stretched and sprawled across the trodden sands.
> The waterline creeps close.

There is a kind of cinematic slow-motion to her ease with the dimming of time—a poet coming to terms with the fragilities of the world and our lives in it. I don't hear the voice of one who recoils from the reality of this approaching stage in her life or is troubled by it, but one who is reconciled and clear-eyed.

It is poetry of shared intimacies, of the solemn note, as well as of the harmonies and discord between body and soul. Intimate daily experience and private grief permeate this haunting collection in which the author at times seems poised in a state of stasis:

> Sometimes these days I fold my hands and sit quietly,
> a good child.

Hardie's work is a poetry of disciplined compression and deep inquiry into her own experiences and into the world around her—she could indeed be 'one of those Zen solitaries / walking the earth, making poems…', as she describes herself in one poem.

That depth is accompanied by clarity, as well as an insightful awareness of the cyclical nature of life; there is a no-nonsense candour to her probing of the heart, mind and spirit. In 'Waning', another poem dealing with the ineluctable passage of time, she tells us that:

> Some days you wake up in July
> By evening it feels like September

And in the same poem there is regretful understanding that it is '… hard to trust life. / All that I love is alive and already dying.'

In similar mood, 'The Satin Gown' has her contemplating the 'quiet hours of passage' in a marriage house, where the 'torn gown hangs there on the wooden page'—an emblem of how transitory and ephemeral all things are.

Landscape is a strong presence in her work and Hardie's is a truly devoted attention to the landscape, a vivid delight and humane interest in the natural world. Her garden, too, seems to stimulate her poetry, providing some of its most telling visual details: in 'Protecting the Buds', a poem about safeguarding young apple trees from the 'fierce intentions' of pillaging birds, she observes:

> '….Winter, half turning,
> waited on spring toiling after.
> The moist air doused thought,
> the bullfinches sat in the thorn hedge, waiting.'

She is, however, as attuned to the domestic interior—that black satin gown on the back of a door—as she is to the 'hawk's plunge through the August dusk / and the rabbit's blooded scream' or the 'smell of cattle on the wind' or 'spring's green sting' (a beautiful phrase).

The discipline of tight form and simple elegance gives poems such as 'Frida Kahlo' their immediacy and force. While Yeats said that 'Men improve with the years', in 'Sixty', Hardie notes 'the hesitant note in his gait/ Where once there was ease and strut'.

The word parable is one that I recall being once used to describe Hardie's poems—it seems an apposite one. These are poems written at a meditative distance; she is a poet of great stillness, the cool gaze, recognising how the sea takes the edge off the land or how:

> All roadsides in the world are unmarked graves
> For those that strife or famine dispossessed.

Hardie is at heart a pastoralist but an uncompromising one who knows what lurks in the shadowlands, and these new poems further underscore that quality. She carries a deep sense of the locale, the rural landscape, out of which she writes. The mood of earlier work—measured and serene—is sustained here but with the added weight of those intimations of time moving on; her landscapes bear evidence of 'the first frost of autumn' or 'the gnaw of winter'.

There is a poem of Robert Frost's about going out to clear the pasture in spring, in which he says to the reader, 'You come too'—but I think in Hardie's case she wants to be afforded the kind of solitude that deepens the experience, and the result of that is a far richer poem and a richer reward for the reader.

Hardie's lyric voice and its bracing power results in poems that are as supple as the named trees in her title poem, 'The Ash and the Oak and the Wild Cherry Tree', in which those trees are 'telling those tales about silence/how it comes when the leaves are gone'—but the poet instead needs the trees 'to tell that other story, / the one that's murmurous with wind and leaves'.

Despite the sense of ennui perceptible in many of the poems, there is an overall life-affirming quality throughout. In a short poem in a previous collection, Kerry Hardie concluded that 'that there is nothing to do in the world except live in it'. Her poems suggest that she does this admirably.

Frank Ormsby is another poet with an understated and unfaltering command of the language of restraint, and in the chorus of poetic voices from the North of Ireland, he might be said to be the quiet one, an almost reticent or reserved voice. It is a characteristic that adds to the attractions of his work—which is not to say he stands in some kind of isolation.

His various collections stack up to an impressive achievement, a singular and memorable body of work that maps out the longitudes and latitudes of the quotidian life, but never neglects wider historical perspective and contexts: historical resonances are never far from daily life in the North where Ormsby, a former editor of that literary stalwart, *The Honest Ulsterman*, has had a long career as a teacher.

Each of his collections has, for the most part, been superbly and daringly assembled, with many of the key poems based around a particular theme that acts as fulcrum to the book.

Fireflies, his most recent collection and which has not received the kind of attention it deserves, adheres to this template. In it, the poet absorbs and renders in a sequence of finely pitched lyrics aspects of the American landscape—in this instance Valhalla in Upstate New York and also regions of the Midwest. He delves into the American experience and idiosyncrasies in a way that, maybe only an outsider, one with perhaps an alien sensibility, can.

It should be added that, while Ormsby's collections have had thematic threads running through them (the birth of his children, the American GIs who passed through the North on their way to the Second World War) each poem firmly stands on its own, and again that is the case with these American settings.

His work has always been approachable and direct. He has been an astute and insightful observer—and recorder—of life in the North, with a particularly focused gaze on the cityscape of Belfast. These gifts of tactful observance are brought into play in these latest mediations on place—'The Kenisco Dam', 'Valhalla Journal', 'Washington's Headquarters', all of them powerfully evocative:

> The Kenisco Dam is brimming with Catskill rains,
> its blocked buttress braced to catch their drift
> in valleys cleared years before we were born.

Reviews

> We skirt the edge and imagine the old town
> nailed to the bottom, its weathercocks askew
> in a climate they never expected…

The American landscape is—'poetically'—a well-trodden one, and poets tackling it have giants on their shoulders; but the keen awareness of place that has been a hallmark of Ormsby's Northern poems is evident here too.

That, and his unshowy expressive powers produce authentic results that capture 'the tone of the landscape'. There is, too, an effortless and fluent shift between his various American settings: 'a hamlet where half the suburbs are cemeteries'; places that have their 'Italian nights, Irish nights, Polish nights'; and what he sees as the 'storm lantern blur of towns on the Hudson'.

He is an exacting poet, but can be playful with his images—as in the title poem, 'Fireflies': 'What should we make of fireflies, their quick flare/of promise and disappointment, their throwaway style?' Or the wonderful homage to American beers, 'At the Lazy Boy Saloon and Ale Bar', with its profusion of witty touches: 'We have travelled a hundred beer-miles past the doors/ of Nat's, Joe's, Mike's, Pat's, Al's where tonight/ they are serving their full range: Bud and Bud Lite. / Neither beer-snobs nor connoisseurs, we roll the names/ like lines from favourite poems…'

In the book's closing section, Ormsby returns to more familiar Northern terrain in 'Blackbirds, North Circular Road' and other poems, but cannot get away from America in his homage to the cowboy movie, 'The Aluminium Box'. The box is one with precious celluloid cargo:

> John Wayne is in it and Clint Walker and Joel McCrea
> And Randolph Scott who never lost his hat,
> Wichita and Dodge City and Boothill.

In 'from City Journal' the poet travels the Carr's Glen Bus on the Cavehill Road and through Royal Avenue carrying the poems of Galway Kinnell 'in the poetry pocket / of my black overcoat'.

Ormsby is indeed a poet well worth finding space for in any poetry pocket. In one of his poems, he speaks of a moon 'that seems to command / definitive utterance/ a clarifying take/ so pure and simple/ no one can understand / it was not obvious'. Definitive utterance—beautifully crafted—and a clarifying take stand at the heart of this fine collection.

—GERARD SMYTH

Replacement
by Tor Ulven (Dalkey Archive, 2012, £8.99)

I met a man on a train journey. He sat down next to me. He was the I'm-going-to-talk-to-you-whether-you-like-it-or-not type.

When he saw I was reading, he chose to kick-start the conversation by announcing that he'd never read a book in his entire life. He said so with such triumph, as though this were a thing to be proud of, an achievement worthy of telling to strangers on trains. During the conversation which followed, the man elaborated on his idea that the reading of books somehow stands in the way of actually living, that it is somehow akin to taking a photograph of a chrysalis only to miss the exact moment when the butterfly emerges. And I argued back with the idea that the reading of books in fact greatly expands all the dull actualities of living, that it pushes me to notice things otherwise unnoticed, then ushers me on into querying them, into needling out their meaning, or meaninglessness, as the case may be.

I suppose I was aiming to imply that the process of noticing and querying and needling is a positive, soul-building exercise, but there was a quaver of doubt in my arguing voice. The book I happened to be reading on the train that day was the sole novel of Tor Ulven, a Norwegian writer born in 1953 and better known for his poetry. I was only in the earliest stages of *Replacement*, and while it had already heightened all the slightest nuances of my surroundings and sharpened all the shadiest corners of my consciousness, still I hadn't the faintest notion of what was going on from page to page. I suppose my voice quavered because I was feeling increasingly despondent the more I advanced upon the afterword.

Here are the essentials of what I was able to grasp: the book's narrator may be the same man all the way through, but is most likely several. At times we are in the present and he is speaking about himself. At other times, he is remembering the past and beseeching me, the reader, to remember too. There is the haunting presence of a woman and the devastation of her absence; 'the combined weight of her disappearance and the high probability of her death rested on a piece of sandpaper that was in the process of whittling you down to nothing.' There are blinks of unforeseen humour by means of arch criticism of society's gormless masses: 'you'd like to kick them out of their couchy quagmires, their sofas with seats like quicksand, sucking them in until all the poor saps can do is to flail about with their arms sticking pathetically out of the cushions.' There are physical descriptions of immense beauty: 'the fatty rind of the day between the hills and the sky finally disappears.' There are several perfect summations of abject grief: 'if you go blind the film will break, and all the darkness that's stored in your eye, and all the darkness stored in your mind's eye, will come flooding out to drown the earth.'

I regret that it's my old-fashioned yet irresistible instinct as a reader to reach out for some rein of a storyline to be drawn along by, for some semblance of continuity. This is how I read the early stages of *Replacement*, and why I grew so quickly bewildered. Some time after the day of the train journey, I twigged that the trick is to concentrate sentence by sentence. Like the old adage of life being best lived one day at a time, *Replacement* is best absorbed in severed strands, passage by passage. It is in pieces that the book bares its fullest force of intensely felt and concisely conjured states and reference points, random though they may be. Whenever I tried to knot them together and abseil to the finish, each of Ulven's individual insights and dark truths were lost to my unforgivable impatience.

Lean in and listen carefully, and the substance of *Replacement* reveals itself to be exactly 'all the dull actualities of living' in their most vividly hideous glory. The tiniest of details, from the act of buttoning and unbuttoning a shirt to a list of doors, swell to crushing enormousness, and Ulven confirms himself an expert in the field of monotony. Leaning in and listening carefully, such is the relentless thrust of detail that I must resist my instincts and relearn the way in which I have grown accustomed to assimilating prose. Ulven pushes me to notice and query and needle, even when I don't really want to, even when it makes me strangely sad and uncomfortable to do so.

Tor Ulven killed himself in 1995, two years after *Replacement* was published, at the still-young-enough-for-it-to-be-considered-a-waste age of forty-two. This is not a thing which matters to the book, per se. But, knowing this, it is hard not to search for signs of the writer's impending self-destruction.

There are many places in the novel where Ulven, by means of his narrator, contemplates death and dying. There is one place in particular where he speaks directly about suicide: 'you remember what the psychiatrist said, how when someone finally convinces themselves to do it, they seem excited, cheerful, they seem happy, energetic, and everyone thinks they're getting better, but in fact they're not getting better, they're just grimly, morbidly happy because they've finally decided to do it…'

Yet the book's most soul-building contemplations arise from the places in which Ulven's narrator bluntly catalogues his struggles with 'all the dull actualities of living', sometimes yielding to the monotony and sometimes battling against: 'You've often wished you could just give up entirely, but that's an inhuman task, you think, because you've got to be a god, or at least a holy man, to simply give up, to resign yourself to the meagre pleasures afforded by the daily grind, though even those pleasures are few and fading, swiftly fading until they're almost out of sight, while you drool—and will most likely go on drooling all the rest of your days—over the last sorry scraps of time, of experience, of life, whatever the hell that means.' It seems to me as though, in these places, Ulven is assembling a case for the continuation of life, (mine, yours, his) and then deftly picking his own case to pieces again, reaching a conclusion of resounding irresolution.

The man on the train and I didn't spend very long on the topic of reading. We lapsed back into our respective silences without convincing one another. I certainly wouldn't have recommended *Replacement*, knowing full well he'd never, without story, without continuity, without reins, have made it all the way through to the afterword. Ulven has written for a reader more open to noticing and querying and needling than the man on the train that day: a reader of gloomy fascinations, a reader inclined toward the occasional indulgence of despondency, a reader in search of the most perfect of reasons for a temporary postponement of actual life.

—SARA BAUME

Winter Journal
by **Paul Auster** (Faber and Faber, 2012, £17.99)

A Death in the Family
by **Karl Ove Knausgaard** (Harvil Secker, 2012, £17.99)

Paul Auster made his first full-length prose appearance with *The Invention of Solitude*, a short memoir written on the occasion of his father's sudden death in 1979. In the first section of the book, 'Portrait of an Invisible Man', Auster recalls rummaging through his father's things and finding a family portrait taken in the 1910s, when his father was no more than a year old. He notices a tear and, later, 'a man's fingertips grasping the torso of one of my uncles.' His grandfather had been torn out of the photograph, which had then been clumsily mended. 'Only his fingertips remain: as if he were trying to crawl back into the picture.' Auster will later discover that his grandmother had murdered her husband, that she'd stood trial, and been acquitted by reason of insanity. The story was kept from the grandchildren, expunged from the Auster family history.

Winter Journal, Auster's latest memoir, opens with the author, now sixty-four years old, looking at himself in the mirror and offering an account of how he received each of the scars on his apparently well-scarred face. He cut his face open at the age of three, for instance, when he collided with a carpenter's nail while belly-flopping along the glassy surface of a Newark department store. The only reason the scarring wasn't much worse, he writes, had something to do with the 'subtle double-stitching method' used by the doctor. Almost all of his scars have their origins in similar misadventures, common to children everywhere. Just one remains a mystery. 'No story accompanies this scar,' he writes, 'your mother never talked about it, and you find it odd, if not downright perplexing, that this permanent line was engraved on your chin by what can only be called an invisible hand, that your body is the site of events that have been expunged from history.'

This 'invisible hand' seems to have crawled straight out of *The Invention of Solitude*, where its fingertips could just about still be seen. That early memoir is further evoked by the scarring motif; for what is a scar if not skin torn, then mended? This is Auster's own 'subtle double-stitching method', which pulls the two books together to form a sort of filial diptych. Any hopes that *Winter Journal* might rank alongside *The Invention of Solitude* are quickly dashed, however. As you may have noticed, *Winter Journal* opens in the second-person singular, a quirk I at first put down to the fact that the narrator had so far spent most of the time standing in front of a mirror. It soon became clear that this was not merely an opening gambit, but a strategy Auster would employ all the way to endgame.

There is nothing inherently wrong with second-person narratives, of course. At its best, the use of the second person can challenge the assumption of a unitary textual subject and have an ultimately destabilising effect upon the narrative in question. Auster manages to do neither. 'We are all aliens to ourselves,' he writes at one point, 'and if we have any sense of who we are, it is only because we live inside the eyes of others.' This is to some extent true, but Auster's use of the second person as his way of 'living inside the eyes of others' feels superficial, slapped on. The judgments the narrator makes about 'you' are no different than those he would have made about 'I'. Had he not spent his career reminding us that he writes using a 1974 Olympia portable typewriter, it would not be in the least surprising to find that the entire text had been written in the first person and later altered using 'find' and 'replace'.

What's most irritating about the second person in this case is that it bestows upon the narrative an air of importance that most of it simply doesn't merit. Sure, there are occasional passages that contain something of the unsettling, preternatural quality found in much of Auster's best work. He visits the site where Bergen-Belsen once stood, for instance, and on the spot marked 'Here lie the bodies of 50,000 Russian soldiers' he experiences the only auditory hallucination of his life: 'A tremendous surge of voices rose up from the ground beneath you, and you heard the bones of the dead howl in anguish, howl in pain, howl in a roaring cascade of full-throated, ear-splitting torment. The earth was screaming. For five or ten seconds you heard them, and then they went silent.' This is undoubtedly good writing. But it would be altogether too kind to dwell on moments such as this when the overwhelming majority of *Winter Journal* occupies a space located somewhere between the sentimental, the smug and the dull-beyond-belief.

In one passage that would not seem out of place in an edition of *Chicken Soup for the Soul*, Auster writes: 'A bit later on, tackle football, Johnny on the Pony, Kick the Can, King of the Castle, Capture the Flag. You and your friends were so nimble, so flexible, so keen on waging these pretend wars that you went at one another with unrelenting savagery, small bodies crash into other small bodies, knick one another to the ground, yanking arms, grabbing necks, tripping and shoving, anything and everything to win the game—animals the lot of you, wild animals through and through. But how well you slept back then. Switch off the lamp, close your eyes… and see you tomorrow.' There is nothing wrong with dull memories per se, but when they are offered up in the second person, the act of remembering (and misremembering) is outsourced and so 'the trembling of existence' arrives only second hand—if it arrives at all.

One recent memoir that illustrates the importance of a strong first-person narrator is *A Death in the Family* by Norwegian novelist Karl Ove Knausgaard. Set against a bleak Norwegian landscape, the memoir jumps between the past and the near-present, as Knausgaard remembers life growing up under the tyrannical reign of his father, an austere and taciturn man who, upon divorcing his wife, became an alcoholic, lost his job as a teacher and moved back in with his mother until he eventually dies as a result of his drinking. When Knausgaard and his brother go to their grandmother's to collect the body, they find the house in a state of squalor, the air thick with the smell of shit.

It's not all quite so extreme, though. Large sections of the book are devoted to the rather mundane efforts Knausgaard made to get stupidly drunk as a teenager. 'I drank, and I became as euphoric as the first time, but on this occasion I had a blackout and remembered nothing between the fifth glass and the moment I woke up in a dark cellar wearing jogging bottoms and a sweatshirt I had never seen before and lying on top of a duvet covered with the towels, my own clothes next to me bundled up and spattered with vomit.' It isn't until his father's later alcoholism is revealed that these remembrances of binges past take on any major significance. The story is framed in such a way that the father seems to inherit his son's alcoholism, something the narrator has known all along. The 'I' sees and is seen—and it is in the space and time between those two roles that the very best memoirs are charged. This is not somewhere I think a second-person narrative can access—certainly not the type Auster has used, in any case. 'You' is seen, but it's not clear that 'you' sees. Even a simple line like Auster's 'you were so nimble' takes on a whole other world of pathos when changed to 'I was so nimble'.

One of the richest aspects of *A Death in the Family* is the way Knausgaard writes about his own experience of visual art. 'That was the only parameter with art,' he writes, 'the feelings it aroused.' Visual art becomes a sort of prism of the narrator's self. His discussion of, say, a Rembrandt self-portrait is itself an exercise in self-portraiture. His meditations on particular paintings or photographs are written to such haunting effect that their memory resonates throughout the text, where they are all put to work, made to comment on theme and form.

His very first memory, for instance, is of seeing 'a very old man with a white beard and white hair', who 'walked with a stick and his back bowed' and whose face he later saw on a poster in his father's office. 'They laughed, and said it was impossible. That's Ibsen, they said. He died nearly a hundred years ago. But I was sure it was the man, and I said so.' The past is forever intruding on the present, in other words, but at the same time memory is fallible, creative, pliable. 'I opened my eyes,' he writes later after his father appears to him. 'I couldn't remember ever experiencing this, it was not a memory, but if it was not a memory, what was it? Oh, no, he was dead.'

Discussing Rembrandt's famous self-portrait of 1663-65, Knausgaard writes: 'The difference between this painting and the others the late Rembrandt painted is the difference between seeing and being seen. That is, in this picture he sees himself seeing while also being seen.' No painting illustrates the possibilities of self-scrutiny afforded the first-person memoirist better than this one does. Rembrandt was not yet sixty years old when he painted it, and yet he appears considerably older and wiser and truer than Paul Auster does aged sixty-four in his misconceived account of getting old. Something to do with the 'I's, I'd say.

—KEVIN BREATHNACH

NOTES ON CONTRIBUTORS

Sara Baume's short story 'Still Turning Slowly' appeared in the Winter 2010-11 issue of *The Stinging Fly*. She writes occasional articles about visual art and books and other haphazard things of interest. She can be found at www.sarabaume.wordpress.com.

Claire-Louise Bennett lives in the west of Ireland where she is bringing together a collection of work called *At The Time Of Writing*. From time to time she posts small things here: magicelbow.blogspot.com

Kevin Breathnach is a recent graduate of Trinity College Dublin, where he studied French and Philosophy. His work has appeared in *The New Inquiry*, *3:AM Magazine* and *Totally Dublin*. He currently lives and works in Gwangju, South Korea.

Colin Corrigan has an MA in Creative Writing from UCD, and his stories have appeared in the Fiction Desk anthology, *All These Little Worlds*, and in the Summer 2011 issue of *The Stinging Fly*. Read his blog at hatsoff.org/blog.

Mary Costello's stories have been anthologised and published in *New Irish Writing* and in *The Stinging Fly*. She received an Arts Council bursary in 2011. *The China Factory*, her debut collection of stories, has been nominated for the Guardian First Book Award.

Ted Deppe has lived in Ireland since 2000 and makes his home in Renvyle, County Galway. His most recent books are *Cape Clear: New and Selected Poems* (Salmon) and *Orpheus on the Red Line* (Tupelo).

Joe Dresner was born in Sunderland in 1987 and currently lives and works in London. He has work published or forthcoming in *Poetry Review*, *Ambit*, *Stand* and *The SHOp*.

Elaine Feeney won the 2008 Cúirt Festival's Poetry Grand Slam. Her chapbook, *Indiscipline*, was published by Maverick Press and in 2010 her first collection, *Where's Katie?*, was published by Salmon Poetry. Elaine's next collection, *The Stinking Rose*, is forthcoming from Salmon in 2013. Her work has been translated into Slovene, Italian and Lithuanian.

Nicola Griffin has lived in East Clare since 1997. In spring 2013 her debut collection of poetry will be published by Salmon and her first non-fiction book will be published by New Island. She received an Arts Council bursary in 2012.

David Hayden's stories have appeared in *The Yellow Nib*, *The Moth* and *The Stinging Fly*. He was shortlisted for the 25th RTE Francis Mac Manus Short Story prize.

Tania Hershman is the author of two story collections: *My Mother Was An Upright Piano: Fictions* (Tangent Books, 2012) and *The White Road and Other Stories* (Salt, 2008). She is writer-in-residence in Bristol University's Science Faculty and editor of *The Short Review*, the online journal spotlighting short story collections and their authors. www.taniahershman.com

Carolyn Jess-Cooke's debut poetry collection, *Inroads* (Seren, 2010), received a number of prizes, including the Tyrone Guthrie Prize for Poetry and a Northern Promise Award. Her debut novel, *The Guardian Angel's Journal* (Piatkus, 2011), is published in twenty-one languages.

Victoria Kennefick, a native of Shanagarry, County Cork, is a poet, writer and teacher. A Fulbright Scholar, she completed a PhD in Literature in 2009. Most recently, she read her work at the Seamus Heaney Poetry Summer School 2012.

Fran Lock's work has previously appeared in *The Stinging Fly*, *Poetry London*, *Blackbox Manifold*, the *Morning Star*, and in anthologies by Little Episodes and Oxfam. Most recently two of her poems were included in *Best British Poetry 2012* (Salt). Her first collection of poems, *Flatrock*, was published last year by Little Episodes.

Clare McCotter trained as a psychiatric nurse in Belfast in the 1980s. In 2005 she was awarded a PhD in literature from the University of Ulster. Her haiku, tanka and haibun have been published in leading short form journals. She was a winner in the Irish Haiku Society International Haiku Competition 2010, and she judged the British Haiku Awards in 2011. Her home is Kilrea, County Derry.

Danielle McLaughlin's stories have appeared in *Inktears*, *Southword*, *The Stinging Fly*, *Boyne Berries*, *Crannóg*, on the RTE TEN website, on RTE Radio and in various anthologies. She won the From the Well Short Story Competition 2012 and the William Trevor/Elizabeth Bowen International Short Story Competition 2012.

Seán Mac Mathúna has published three novels in Irish, *Hulla Hul* (Leabhar Breac), *Scéal Eitleáin* (Coiscéim) and *Gealach* (Leabhar Breac). His poetry collections in Irish, *Ding* (Edco) and *Banana* (Cois Life) won him acclaim, and his English collection, *The Atheist* (Wolfhound), was nominated by the Arts Council for the European Prize in Literature. His play, *The Winter Thief/ Gadaí Géar*, was produced by the Abbey Theatre.

Gina Moxley is a writer, actor and director. Her most recent play was *The Crumb Trail* for Pan Pan Theatre. Two of her plays, *Danti-Dan* and *Dog House*, are published by Faber and Faber. She recently directed *Solpadeine is My Boyfriend* and *The Wheelchair on My Face*, which won a Fringe First at the 2012 Edinburgh Festival. Her story, 'Cuts', appeared in the anthology, *Let's Be Alone Together* (Stinging Fly Press, 2008).

Stiofán Ó Cadhla was born in Ring, County Waterford, and was raised both there and in Bishopstown in Cork city. He is Head of the Department of Folklore and Ethnology, University College Cork. His first collection, *An Creidmheachach Déanach* (Coiscéim 2009), was awarded the Michael Hartnett Memorial Prize in 2012 and his second, *Tarraing na Cuirtíní, a Dhochtúir* (Coiscéim 2012), was given a prize of merit in Comórtas Literary an Oireachtais 2012.

Fiona O'Connor teaches creative writing at the University of Westminster, London. She produces theatre in Kerry. As part of the 400th anniversary celebrations of Puck Fair in Killorglin next summer, she is directing an open-air production of Shakespeare's *The Tempest*.

John O'Donnell has won various awards for poetry and has also published two poetry collections. His first published short story, 'Promise', was shortlisted for the Hennessy Awards in 2010. This is his first story in *The Stinging Fly*.

Ruth Padel's latest collection is *The Mara Crossing*, a mixed-genre reflection of migration (cells, plants, animals and human beings) in poems and prose. See www.ruthpadel.com.

Paul Perry is a poet and fiction writer. His most recent book is *The Last Falcon and Small Ordinance* (The Dedalus Press, 2010). With Karen Gillece, he has written *The Innocent Sleep*, a 'Karen Perry' thriller to be published by Penguin (UK) and Henry Holt (USA) in 2014.

Suzanne Power's novels have sold rights to territories worldwide. Her two most recent books were non-fiction. This year she has produced short stories and poetry which have been published in various collections. 'Pilgrimage' was written as an outcome of the Coracle international writers' professional development residency. This residency was part funded by the European Regional Development Fund through the Ireland Wales Interreg 4a programme. www.coracle.eu.com

Sally Rooney is a final-year student of English at Trinity College Dublin. She previously had poetry published in the Spring 2010 issue of *The Stinging Fly*.

J. Roycroft's work has appeared in *The SHOp*, *Flaming Arrows*, and *The Burning Bush 2*, amongst others. Educated at Queen's University, Belfast, he lives with his wife and two children in Dublin. He is currently at work on the companion novels, *The Imitation Game* and *In Fiction*.

S.J. Ryan was born in England and has lived in South Africa, Ireland and the Caribbean. A lawyer by profession, she is pursuing a PhD in Creative Writing at Aberystwyth University. She has been published in *The Stony Thursday Book* and is currently working on several short stories and an historical novel.

Janet Shepperson lives in Belfast. Her poetry collections are *The Aphrodite Stone* (Salmon Poetry, 1995) and *Eve Complains to God* (Lagan Press, 2004). She has also published short stories, two of which were shortlisted for Hennessy Awards.

K.V. Skene's recent publications include *You Can Almost Hear Their Voices* (Indigo Dreams Publishing, 2010). After eighteen years as an expat in England and Ireland, K.V. is now repatriated and writes from Toronto, Canada.

Gerard Smyth has published seven collections of poetry, the latest of which is *The Fullness of Time: New and Selected Poems* (Dedalus Press, 2010). He was the recipient of this year's O'Shaughnessy Poetry Award from the University of St Thomas in Minnesota and is a member of Aosdána.

Haris Vlavianos is the author of ten collections of poetry in Greek. He lives in Athens, where he teaches History and Political Theory at the American College of Greece, and is editor of the journal, *Poetics*. [**Evan Jones** is a Canadian poet who has lived in Manchester since 2005. His second collection, *Paralogues*, is published by Carcanet.]

Grace Wells was our Featured Poet in Issue 10 Volume Two, Summer 2008. Her debut collection, *When God Has Been Called Away to Greater Things* (Dedalus Press, 2010), won the Rupert and Eithne Strong Award and was shortlisted for the London Festival Fringe New Poetry Award.

Lou Wilford lives in South Yorkshire where she is currently working as a private tutor and freelance writer, and studying for a BSc in Psychology. She has had work published in many poetry magazines including *The Stinging Fly, Agenda, The Coffee Room, Iota, OWP, Equinox, Staple* and *Aspire*. She has been shortlisted twice for the Bridport Prize and once for the Templar Poets anthology competition. She is working on a fantasy novel.

Subscribe to The Stinging Fly

Three issues: €20 IRL & NI / €25 overseas

Six issues: €36 IRL & NI / €45 overseas

Pay online via paypal at www.stingingfly.org

Pay by bank transfer – instructions on our website

Send a cheque/postal order to:

The Stinging Fly, PO Box 6016, Dublin 1, Ireland

Keep in touch: sign up to our e-mail newsletter, become a fan on Facebook, or follow us on Twitter for regular updates about all our publications, events and activities.

www.stingingfly.org | www.facebook.com/StingingFly | @stingingfly